HERE'S
ARE S/

KEITH A. ROBINSON'S
ORIGINS TRILOGY:

Logic's End is a great read, and I highly recommend it. It explores the question of what life would be like on a planet where evolution really did happen. The surprising result helps the reader to see why life on Earth must be the result of special creation. For those interested in science fiction but who are tired of all the evolutionary nonsense, *Logic's End* is a refreshing alternative.

—Jason Lisle, PhD, Astrophysicist
Institute for Creation Research

In this book, Robinson has discovered a 'novel' way to communicate vital information to young adults and readers of all ages. Mainstream indoctrination on the origin of species and the age of the earth are regularly encountered and have long needed combating. Through this unique story, truth is conveyed.

—Dr. John D. Morris President
Institute for Creation Research

Pyramid of the Ancients will challenge you to reconsider the conventional wisdom concerning the history of our world.

—Tim Chaffey, Writer/Speaker
Answers in Genesis, Co-author of
Old-Earth Creationism on Trial

Escaping the Cataclysm is an edge-of-your-seat thrill ride back through time. It brilliantly explains the plausibility of the biblical account of history, especially Noah's Flood. It also explores details of the feasibility of the Ark itself and the Flood's impact on the earth. A great read!

—Julie Cave
Author of *The Dinah Harris Mysteries series*

Picking up where *Pyramid of the Ancients* leaves off, *Escaping the Cataclysm* hits the ground with both feet running. I found my faith renewed again and again as I was reminded of the many arguments that demonstrate why evolution cannot be the explanation for our origins.

—Joe Westbrook
Co-author of *The Truth Chronicles*

ELYSIUM

TARTARUS CHRONICLES BOOK 1

ELYSIUM

KEITH A. ROBINSON

Cover Artwork by Jaslynn Tham

Published in the United States of America

ISBN 10: 1548231622

ISBN 13: 9781548231620

1. Fiction / Christian / General

2. Fiction / Dystopian

Novels by
Keith A. Robinson

The Origins Trilogy

Book 1: *Logic's End*
Book 2: *Pyramid of the Ancients*
Book 3: *Escaping the Cataclysm*

The Tartarus Chronicles

Book 1: *Elysium*
Book 2: *Dehali*
Book 3: *Bab al-Jihad*
Book 4: *Labyrinth*

The Master Symphony Trilogy

Book 1: *Prelude and Abduction in A Minor*
Book 2: *Fugue for the Sacred Songbook in Eb Minor*
Book 3: *March of the Free in C Major*

CONTENTS

PROLOGUE

The first sign of its appearance was the slight movement of air. In the complete stillness of the cavern, even the smallest breeze was noticeable. A haggard man sat on the rough floor, his back leaning against the wall of gleaming purple-colored rock. His eyes flew open in excitement as the first tendril of wind brushed past his face.

He stood and scanned the small cavern. Hope sent adrenaline coursing through his veins. Movement to his left captured his attention. His eyes grew wide and his pulse quickened at the sight of the strange purple mist swirling near the far wall.

"It's forming! It's forming!" he screamed at the top of his lungs. His words echoed off the glowing walls long after his voice had ceased. An expression of panicked excitement quickly replaced the hopeless, vacant look that had almost permanently creased his forty-year-old face.

The purple mist thickened as it swirled tighter and tighter into a circular shape. The man was oblivious to the excited voices and trampling feet which were gradually increasing in volume. His attention was completely captured by the ever-expanding circle.

The anomaly had reached twenty feet in diameter. Although the edges still retained their gaseous form, the inner disc turned black and seemed to bend as if being pulled toward the wall of the cavern by some invisible hand. Threads of color and light worked their way from the center of the disc outward toward the edges.

The lone spectator of the bizarre event inched forward, his long hair and ragged clothing thrashing in the wind created by the swirling mist. When he drew within six feet of the anomaly, he stopped and crouched. His muscles tensed like a large predatory cat preparing to pounce on its prey.

Three tiny figures suddenly appeared within the center of the disc. They grew from mere inches in height to full size within a matter of seconds. The human bodies tumbled out of the black disc and fell to the ground at the man's feet. Yet before they had even struck the floor of the cavern, he let out a cry of victory and leapt over the newcomers toward the anomaly.

A crowd of men and women burst through the cavern opening and watched as he came in contact with the swirling disc. His body flew backward to land in a heap several feet away. Despite what they had just witnessed, the crowd cried out in desperation and ran toward the disturbance.

The screaming mob roused the three figures lying on the cold stone floor. Dazed, they stared in shock at the wild men and women rushing toward them. The trio huddled close together with their faces averted, terror griped their hearts.

However, the crazed men and women completely ignored them. They threw themselves at the circle of blackness only to meet the same fate as the first man. Within moments, the cavern was filled with bodies tossed aside by the swirling mist. Then, as quickly as it had appeared, the mist dissipated and dissolved until not a single trace remained.

The occupants of the cavern remained motionless, as if frozen in time. A soft weeping broke the stillness. Other anguished voices joined in until the whole cavern reverberated with the sounds of sobbing and grieving.

The three newcomers, a man and two women, continued to hug one another with their eyes closed tightly in a vain effort to shut out the sights and sounds of this nightmare.

"That's enough!"

The strength contained in those two simple words instantly quelled the tumult. Every eye in the room was drawn toward the speaker. He stood over six feet in height and was strongly built. However, even without his imposing physique, he had an inner strength that demanded respect and exuded authority. Unlike many of the others, his clothes were better kept and were of a higher quality.

"How long are we going to go on like this?" he asked, his voice echoing in the chamber. "Since my wife and I first arrived here four years ago, we've tried everything we could think of to get the portals to take us back. I understand you haven't been here as long as we have, and I know you want to try everything you can to escape from here. But we need to face the horrible truth: for the time being, this is now our home."

The sounds of muffled crying began anew. The man continued speaking. As he did so, he walked around the gathering and laid a gentle touch on the heads or shoulders of the others like a shepherd comforting his flock. "Don't get me wrong, we will continue to search for ways home. We will have the wisest among us study these portals to find a way to reverse them. Others will be given the task of exploring the cave system in hopes of finding a way to reach the surface."

A man rose to his feet and held his hands out imploringly, his face filled with raw emotion. "What good will that do, Mathison? This hellish place is filled with strange animals no one has ever seen before, glowing purple rock, rivers filled with fish that shine. We can't…we can't *possibly* still be on Earth. So even if we reach the surface, that won't put us any closer to home!"

"You may be right," Mathison replied. "But we must still explore. If we *have* been brought here by aliens, as many of us believe, then perhaps we can find them and seek their help to return to Earth. Either way, we have to map our surroundings to make sure that nothing—animal or alien—will catch us by surprise. Whether we like it or not, we are pioneers facing a new frontier, and we will either pull together or die."

Mathison paused, letting his words hang in the air and sink into their souls. "But do not despair! Although I long to return home, I would disagree that this place is 'hellish.' It may be unfamiliar to us, but only a blind man would fail to see the beauty of this world! We may be underground, but we have everything we need—water, plants, and numerous raw materials. Together, we can build a new world. When we do finally find a way to reverse the portals, we will have already built an outpost from which others can launch further explorations."

A woman leaning against the wall lifted her head and glared at him, her face wet with tears. "You and your grandiose plans! What good will they do if we all go insane? Or have you forgotten what happened to Kaylee and Michael, the McCrary boys, or any of the other friends we've known who've committed suicide or gone mad from being trapped here? And what about the new diseases we discovered? And how many more young people are we going to lose as they go exploring? This place is no wonderful 'frontier'. It's a punishment! It *is* hell! It is Tartarus—a prison!"

"No!" Mathison snapped. Several of those nearest him started in surprise. Realizing what he had just done, he took a deep breath and allowed a gentle smile to soften his features. "Julie, I know you still grieve for your children, but don't you see that by focusing on building a new life, we will have purpose! We'll have a goal! This will help prevent madness. And the more we learn about this world, the more we can prevent diseases and accidents. But in order to do that, we need the expertise of everyone, including all new arrivals."

As he spoke, he walked toward the trio that had appeared from the mist. They were still huddled close together with heads lowered, the man's arms wrapped protectively around the two women. Mathison crouched and laid his hands gently on the shoulders of the man. "Don't be afraid. I know this is all so frightening and new, but you're among friends. My name is George." He stood and looked toward two women sitting nearby. "Alyssa, Emily, please take these three to your cave and give them something to eat." The two women exchanged brief apprehensive glances, then did as instructed.

Once the five of them exited the cavern, Mathison continued. "For the sake of those still coming through the portals, we have to pull ourselves together. You remember when you first came through—the shock of the portal travel and the unfamiliar faces and surroundings. Then, there was the horror of learning the truth that you cannot return. It can be psychologically damaging, especially if we act like fools every time a portal opens. We need to learn how to soften the blow to those just arriving to minimize the effects."

Holding out his arms to encompass his people, George Mathison looked toward the glowing ceiling of the cavern. "Come, my friends. Today is a new day! Today, we take our first step toward creating a new future! We will succeed!"

1

RIFTS

"You're going to end up like my father! Just another deadbeat drunk!"

Braedon's anger flared at his wife's verbal jab, enhanced by the alcohol coursing through his body. He grabbed her arm roughly and brought his face within inches of hers. She flinched in pain, but he kept up the pressure. A twisted area of his soul relished the feeling of power.

"Don't ever say that to me again!" he growled. He released her arm with a shove, causing her to lose balance. She tripped and fell to the carpet of the rental cabin in which they were staying. "For crying out loud, Cat, we're on vacation! I decide to have a couple of drinks and suddenly I'm a drunk!"

Catrina picked herself off the floor and moved behind the nearby recliner. "But this is the third time in the four days we've been here! And you didn't just have a 'few' drinks. You're drunk. You stink, and you're wearing the military fatigues you put on yesterday. How can you stand wearing the same thing every day! It's disgusting!"

"That's life in the military, babe," Braedon shot back with a sneer. "I'd think you'd be used to it after four years of marriage. Don't act so surprised. You knew what you were gettin' into." The fear and regret in her eyes only served to fuel his frustration. He let out a feral growl and stumbled toward the door.

"Where are you going?"

"Out!"

"But…but what about the…portals?"

Braedon responded by slamming the door.

He stomped into the forest surrounding the cabin, his thoughts roiling like storm-tossed waves. *She always makes me the bad guy! She's always comparing me to her jerk of a father! I relax a little and suddenly I'm a drunk and a slob! I never should've married her. High school sweethearts. Hah! What a joke!*

He stumbled and caught himself by leaning against a near-by tree. The sunlight was fading, deepening the shadows. Cat's last statement wormed its way through his addled mind. The portals.

Despite his drunken state, the constant warnings from the news media surfaced. The first incident happened fourteen years ago. Since then, sightings of the mysterious swirling vortexes had increased and remained steady. Nearly all were in secluded areas, such as forests. That was why he and Cat had been able to get such a great deal on the cabin rental. Superstition was definitely bad for business for those in rural areas.

According to the "experts", there was no rhyme or reason to the appearances. Video footage from cell phones from thousands of terrifying encounters showed purple tendrils of light, mist and fog. Eventually the portals took shape, spinning and churning toward a bright center. Anyone unfortunate enough to be in the vicinity was dragged screaming into the void, never to be seen again.

To say that Cat had been frightened to stay at the cabin would be an understatement. But Braedon reassured her. They would stay close and not wander into the woods. Besides, according to the local authorities, there hadn't been any trace of the portals in this area for over a year.

"I'm a soldier, and the son of a soldier," he mumbled aloud, his words slurring. "I'm not afraid of anything. Especially not some mystical light show." His mind set, he continued down the trail.

Braedon returned to the cabin two hours later to find Cat sitting on the bed, her arms wrapped around her knees. Her eyes were red and puffy. Her face streaked with tears. He could read both relief and uncertainty in her expression.

He stopped in the doorway of the bedroom and took in a deep breath. "Cat, I'm…I'm really sorry. I shouldn't have yelled at you."

Cat's expression shifted. A glimmer of hope appeared in her swollen eyes. "I've been so worried. Where did you go? I thought maybe…"

Braedon crossed over and sat on the edge of the bed. He reached out tentatively and placed his hand on her knee. "I just needed some fresh air. I'm feeling better now, but my head hurts. I need to sleep. I found this beautiful river not far from here. There's a bridge, and the view is spectacular. I want to take you tomorrow."

Catrina withdrew from his touch and stood. "We can talk about it later. Get some sleep." She strode toward the door. She stopped and turned toward him. "I'm glad you're okay. Goodnight." She closed the door behind her, leaving Braedon alone with his thoughts.

He awakened the next morning to the heavenly aroma of pancakes and sausages. His stomach, though still struggling with the aftereffects of the alcohol, reminded him he hadn't eaten for over half a day.

He dressed quickly and made his way into the kitchen area. Catrina greeted him with a slight smile. He could see the tension still in her shoulders, and her posture was rigid. Guilt washed over him at his actions the previous night. He had to make it up to her.

"Good morning, beautiful," he leaned in and kissed her hair. "I don't deserve you. You really are an amazing woman."

Her smile deepened. "You're right on both accounts." She flipped some pancakes from the skillet onto a nearby plate next to a trio of sausages. "The syrup's on the table."

Catrina prepared a plate for herself, then sat across from Braedon at the small table. After they had finished eating, Braedon cleared his throat. "Listen, babe. I've been thinking about my actions last night. There's no excuse for what I did. My father was a hard man. I loved him, but he was also the source of much of my own pain. I want to hold on to the good things he taught me, but get rid of the bad. So, I'm going to throw out all the alcohol right now. The rest of our stay here will be free of the stuff."

Her expression lifted. "Really? That would be…nice. But don't make a promise you're not going to keep."

Braedon stood and went directly to his stash. "Then I'll prove it to you." He withdrew the bottles and, one by one, poured their contents down the sink. A part of him lamented the loss of the money it cost to purchase them, but the rekindled light in his wife's eyes far overshadowed those thoughts

"There. It's done," he said as he set the last of the empty bottles onto the counter. He felt Catrina's arms wrap around him from behind. Her cheek came to rest against his back. "I love you, Braedon. We're going to make it, right? We may be broken, but together we can find a way to help each other heal."

Braedon twisted around and cupped her face in his hands. "You bet. The two of us against the world!" He kissed her tenderly. "Now let's do some sightseeing. The sun is up, and the weather is perfect. I've got to show you this place I found last night."

Uncertainty spread once more across her features. "I don't know. Are you sure it's safe?"

"Hon, you know how the media are. They're always trying to scare people in order to improve their ratings. Besides, we're together. Like I said, it's us against the world!

"Catrina brushed a lock of red hair out of her face and nodded. "Okay. Let me just grab a few things."

Ten minutes later they strolled hand in hand down the trail Braedon had discovered the previous night. Before long the comforting sounds of gently flowing water reached their ears. Braedon relished the feel of the sun on his skin. They left the trail and stepped onto the banks of a wide river. Multitudes of colorful flowers sparkled in the sunlight. Bright green grass blanketed the ground and eventually gave way to white sand.

Catrina sucked in a breath. "It's magnificent! I've seen pictures of places like this, but they don't even come close to capturing the true beauty of it."

Braedon led her down to the water's edge. They took off their shoes and socks and waded into the water. Braedon had never felt so alive. The weather was perfect, the peace and calm of the river soothed his mind, and the glimmer in his wife's dazzling green eyes ignited a fire within him.

Cat was right. We're going to make it.

They returned to the bank a while later and laid down on a large rock that stuck out into the water. Braedon closed his eyes and soaked in the rays of the sun. He sighed contentedly as Catrina snuggled at his side. A gentle breeze rustled his hair and brushed his skin.

His first indication something was wrong was when Catrina shivered. Only then did he notice the breeze had turned bitter and cold.

Braedon opened his eyes and sat up. "Did you feel that? It was like…" The words stuck in his throat. A slight purplish hue colored Catrina's face as she sat up next to him. Terror gripped his heart as he turned slowly back toward the bank of the river.

A purplish mist blanketed the entire area and was creeping toward them. The rays of sunlight that managed to make their way through the mist only served to deepen the shadows that fell around them and enhance the ghostly feel of the surrounding area. The former beauty of the flowers and water seemed transformed into twisted, horrible reflections of their true natures.

"Braedon," Catrina gasped. She gripped his arm painfully. "We've got to get out of here!"

Braedon scanned the area and felt his heart sink. They were trapped on the rock. The mist obscured the forest and covered most of the river bank. In front of them lay the swiftly moving current of water.

The air itself suddenly seemed to come alive. The purplish fog began to swirl as crackles of energy became visible. Time slowed to a crawl as the speed of the swirling tendrils of air increased. Braedon turned his head slowly to look at his wife. He could see she was caught in the same time-bending effect.

As if in a warped nightmare, Braedon could feel an unseen force pull at his body. A panicked scream, distorted by the roar of the wind and the crackling energy, escaped from Catrina's lips. Braedon reached out and tried to grab his wife's outstretched hands which clawed desperately at the rock on which they sat.

Acting on instinct, Braedon grabbed his wife's shoulders and threw her as hard as he could toward the river. He fell backward onto the rock. A loud splash came from below. He gasped for air as the tempo of the swirling air around him continued to increase. He strained against the pull and looked toward the river to see Catrina floating with the current. She was going to make it.

Tears welled in his eyes. "I love you, Cat. I'm…I'm so sorry." The whispered words were drowned out by the roaring winds. He slowly turned his head to look behind him and gasped in shock.

What he saw and felt at that moment would be the source of nightmares for years to come. Like water swirling into a whirlpool or flowing through an open drain, the mist spiraled around him toward a central opening of darkness. Braedon felt himself being pulled toward the eye of the tornado-like whirlwind. His mind screamed at the prospect of being sucked into that gaping maw. Try as he might, his body refused to obey his frantic commands. Finally, after what seemed like an eternity of waiting upon a horrific precipice, Braedon fell toward the blackness.

2

THE WELCOME CENTER

"… beginning to come around…"

Although Braedon could hear the muffled words, his mind struggled to comprehend their meaning. He felt himself moving smoothly, as if he were floating. In fact, due to his muddled senses, he wasn't sure if he *might* be floating.

He opened his eyes, but the images transported from his eyes to his brain didn't make any sense. Light filled his vision. *Am…am I…dead?* The phrase slowly formed itself in Braedon's thoughts. "Am…I in…heaven?" he mumbled aloud.

To his surprise, a voice beside him answered softly, "In heaven…and in hell."

Braedon blinked several times, trying once again to make sense of the shadows surrounding him. He appeared to be on his back and either floating or rolling on some kind of bed. On each side were the out of focus but unmistakable shapes of people.

Before he could form another coherent question, a gentle hand came to rest upon his shoulder. "Just try to relax. You're going to be fine."

Braedon searched his memory for anything that might help him figure out what was going on. However, his mind still seemed to be sluggish and unresponsive.

Once again, the calming voice spoke, "We've given you a mild sedative to help ease you through the transition…" If there was anything more to the voice's comments, they were lost to him.

After an indeterminate amount of time, he opened his eyes once more. He was no longer moving, and he could think more clearly. Based on the myriad beeping machines located nearby and the sterile smell hanging in the air, he realized he was in some kind of hospital or medical center. He could hear the hushed voices of the medical staff just outside the door leading into the room. He barely had time to take in his surroundings when a pleasant young nurse entered.

"Good afternoon," she said with a smile. "How are you feeling?"

Braedon, still groggy and confused, answered the question simply. "I've been better."

"I bet," she replied. "But don't worry. The effects of the transition are temporary. We'll have you back on your feet in no time. Now that you're awake, and since all your tests have come back fine, we're going to take you over to the Welcome Room, where all your questions will be answered."

Not knowing what else to say, Braedon remained silent as the nurse helped him out of the hospital bed and into a wheelchair. As she did so, he noticed he wasn't dressed in a typical hospital gown but in simple khaki pants and a plain, light-green shirt with short sleeves.

The nurse guided his wheelchair out the door and down a non-descript hallway. After passing through several sets of double doors, she brought Braedon through a final set of doors into a beautifully decorated room with the words "WELCOME!" written in bold letters across one wall. The room was painted a warm blue with lighter highlights sponged over the walls to create texture. A six-foot, oval-shaped table filled the center of the small room with plush chairs surrounding it. The walls were covered with colorful paintings and designs that seemed to instantly put the mind at ease. To the left of the entrance was a comfortably sized projection screen. Most of the opposite wall was covered by closed curtains. Sculptures and statues were tastefully arranged around the room to add to the overall welcoming atmosphere.

Despite still feeling disoriented and confused, the aesthetics of the room eased his tension. The nurse helped him into one of the plush chairs. Once he was seated, he took a deep breath and sank into the inviting cushion.

Mere moments after the nurse exited the room with the wheel-chair, three men dressed in navy-blue dress pants and matching polo shirts entered, one holding a thin tablet computer under his arm. The man with the tablet smiled warmly at Braedon and sat in the chair directly across from him. The other two men sat near the door. Although their expressions were pleasant enough, something about the way they carried themselves made Braedon feel uneasy.

"Hello. My name is Charles," the smiling man said as he offered his hand to Braedon. Out of ingrained politeness, Braedon shook the man's hand and mumbled a soft hello in return. "I know you have a lot of questions," Charles continued, "and we'll do our best to answer as many of them as we can. But as a matter of protocol, we need to ask a few questions first."

Braedon simply nodded.

"What is your full name?"

"Braedon Gerard Lewis."

"What is your birthdate, including the year?" Charles asked, his fingers working frantically as he took notes on the tablet.

"November 20th, 2022."

"What is the current date, including the year?" In response to Braedon's confused expression, Charles smiled again and said, "Just humor me, please?"

Braedon frowned, but answered the question, "May 15th, 2046."

"What is your occupation?"

"I'm a private in the US Army," Braedon replied with the tone of one who had repeated this phrase thousands of times.

Charles raised his head at the response. "Very good."

The questioning continued for another ten minutes, with Braedon growing increasingly impatient at the mundane nature of the questions. Finally, Charles turned off his tablet and looked at Braedon, a smile once more plastered onto his face.

"Thank you again for your patience. We're sorry for the length and details of the questions, but as you will see soon, they are quite necessary. Now, if you'll turn your attention to the screen, we'll begin the Welcome Vid."

As one of the other men dimmed the lights, Braedon looked intently at Charles. "Welcome Vid? Where am I?"

By way of reply, his host simply pointed forward.

The image of an immaculately dressed man in his mid-fifties filled the screen. He was sitting at a mahogany desk surrounded by beautiful furnishings. Braedon cast one last disturbed look at Charles, then sat back in his chair and listened as the man in the video spoke.

"Hello. My name is Devyn Mathison, and I want to take this opportunity to officially welcome you. While I know you have many questions and are probably very confused right now, let me assure you every effort has been made to make you as comfortable as possible and to minimize the side effects of your recent trip.

"When you first arrived, we administered a mild tranquilizer to ease your discomfort, and you were immediately transported to our Welcome Center. Here you were placed under the professional care of our trained medical specialists, who made sure you suffered no physical trauma. If you don't remember much of this, don't worry. Through extensive surveys of our past guests, we have determined this is by far the best way to reduce stress during your transition.

"Now let me tell you an amazing story—one in which you have the privilege of participating. Over two hundred years ago, a man by the name of George Mathison, my ancestor, was walking through the woods one day with his wife, Jennifer, when the two of them suddenly found themselves transported to a wondrous new world full of beauty and splendor. Before long, others arrived, as if chosen by divine selection to take part in setting up a new colony. As the years passed, this First Colony thrived and grew as additional travelers came through the portals. The more they explored this new world, the more amazing things they uncovered—new species of animals, new types of plants and minerals, and incredible, breathtaking vistas.

"Decades later, they set up cities and a government. Then fifty-two years after the establishment of the First Colony, they discovered others had arrived in different parts of the world and formed cities of their own. Eventually, travel and trade between these new territories increased, and everyone prospered. And now, almost two hundred years since the First Colony, there are six known territories—Elysium, the European States, Dehali, New China, Bab al-Jihad, and the United African Nations.

"And now, it is my honor to explain how you fit in. You see, you were chosen to come here by the Forces that control the portals. If you search your memory, you may remember a purplish mist, swirling wind, and electricity. Rest assured. Although that event may have frightened you, it was simply the method by which you were transported here. And if you were in the company of others when the portal was opened, you will be relieved to know they are safe here as well, very possibly watching this same video even now! Once you are finished with the welcome and orientation, you will see them again."

Braedon felt his gut wrench. *If I hadn't pushed Cat into the water, she'd be here with me now. Instead...*

The video continued, oblivious to his emotional trauma. "In addition, the portal also brought you forward into time. Since George Mathison first arrived in 2008, one hundred and nine-ty-two years have passed. By your reckoning, it is currently the year 2200. So as you explore, you will find some new, exciting tech-nologies awaiting you.

"We believe you were brought here with a purpose. Each person has a unique role to play and special skills to be used for the benefit of everyone. But that is a conversation for another time. For now, you are our guest. As the governor of this territory, let me be the first to officially welcome you. On behalf of our citizens, we want you to relax and explore the wonders of Elysium!"

A flurry of soaring notes played by a symphony orchestra ac-companied the smiling image of Devyn Mathison as the video faded to black. Charles turned to face his guest. "I'm sure you're very excited to begin the tour. But first, I would like to show you what the city looks like from this vantage point. You see, the Wel-come Center was built specifically to provide the most amazing view of the city. Please step over to the window."

Braedon stood numbly. His mind reeled as he tried to process all he had heard. The lingering effects of the sedative made his head swim.

"Brace yourself, Mr. Lewis, for your first glimpse of Elysium!" Charles said with a dramatic flair.

The curtain opened and Braedon gasped in awe. The room in which he stood was hundreds of feet from the ground. He could easily see over the tops of most of the sleek buildings comprising the city. Majestic towers and skyscrapers formed the heart of the metropolis, backed by what appeared to be a mountain range made of simmering purple rock. Surrounding the central buildings were miles upon miles of smaller homes, shops, and businesses. Vehicles of all shapes and sizes moved along the streets and highways dividing the city. To his right, Braedon could see a wide river of pale blue that seemed to glimmer with its own light. Another wall of rock stood a short distance away from the river's far bank. The entire scene was illuminated by a bright light coming from above. He shielded his eyes from the glare and frowned.

"What's the matter with the sun?" Braedon asked. "The color seems off." He sucked in a breath as his mind caught up with his senses. "Wait a second, that's not the sun at all! It's … it's a huge globe!" Turning away from the window, he stared intently at Charles. The two other men in the room rose from their chairs, their posture alert. "This entire city is underground, isn't it? That… that thing hanging there is supposed to simulate the sun!"

Charles lifted his hands, attempting to calm his guest. "Mr. Lewis, there are many things about Elysium that will come as a shock to you."

"You've got that right, genius," Braedon replied. Like cold water suddenly thrown in his face, the newly heightened emotions served to throw off the last effects of the sedative. His recent memories returned in a rush.

"Please, Mr. Lewis, why don't you sit down?"

Braedon took a deep, calming breath. *Take it easy, buddy. It won't do any good losing your cool.* He nodded and returned to his chair, his head bowed low. "There's just so much to take in."

Charles placed a hand on Braedon's shoulder. "I understand. But don't worry. Most people adjust to life here rather quickly."

Braedon's head snapped up. "Adjust? What are you talking about? I don't want to 'adjust.' I want to return home to my wife. I'm not staying here," Braedon stated, his voice rising.

Charles's expression hardened slightly. "I'm sorry, Mr. Lewis, but I'm afraid that won't be possible."

"What? There's gotta be a way out of here!" His grip on the arms of his chair tightened.

"The truth is, no one even knows exactly where we are," Charles explained. "Yes, we're underground, but believe it or not, in the past one hundred and ninety-two years since the arrival of the First Colony, people have been exploring and attempting to tunnel in all directions, hoping to reach the surface. But all efforts have proved futile."

"But what about the swirling purple gas—or whatever it was—that brought me here?" Braedon asked, standing once again.

Charles shook his head sadly as he faced his guest. "Our best scientists have been working for years to find a way to reverse the flow of the wormholes generated by the portals. None have yet succeeded. Mr. Lewis, this may not be easy for you to accept, but Elysium is now your home."

"No," Braedon said softly in disbelief. "No. I can't stay here. My wife…I have to get back home to my wife." He turned and headed toward the door.

The two men moved to block Braedon's path. His combat training kicked in and he swung a fist at the nearest man. However, whether due to the travel through the portal or the lingering effects of the sedative, his motions were clumsy and awkward. The men grabbed him by the arms with practiced skill. Braedon growled in fury, but soon gave in to the inevitable. He was in no condition to fight.

Charles gave him a sympathetic look. "I'm sorry, Mr. Lewis. The life you once knew is now gone. The sooner you forget the past and accept the future, the sooner you will be whole again. We are your family now. Embrace your new life."

Braedon reeled. His thoughts seemed trapped in a deepening pit of negativity and self-recrimination. He was the one that pushed Cat to go to the cabin, to visit the river. And the unthinkable had occurred. Now he would likely never see her again. *If only I had listened to Cat... If only...*

3

A NEW LIFE

The automatic door to Braedon's room inside the Welcome Center opened. A Latina woman strode through the opening, a tablet cradled in her arms.

"Good morning, Mr. Lewis."

Braedon allowed his gaze to drift from the TV screen he had been watching toward the woman. She looked to be in her mid to late twenties with dark eyes and hair. She was pretty, but had an air about her that put him on guard. *Then again, everything about this place puts me on guard.*

He turned his gaze back to the TV as he replied. "If you say so. You guys have kept me caged in this place for over a week now. It's hard to find anything 'good' about the morning when you're a prisoner."

Out of the corner of his eye he saw her face brighten with a smile. "You'll change your opinion when you hear the news I bring."

Her mysterious statement drew his attention. "Yeah?" he asked, his eyebrow lifting. "And what might that be?"

"First of all, my name is Esmeralda, Fourth Gen. I'm your Ac-climation Liaison."

"Fourth Gen?"

She nodded. "As in 'Fourth Generation'. Here in Elysium, when we introduce ourselves, we find it helpful to state when we, or our families, arrived in Tartarus. It gives a point of connection and, in cases of First Gens, like yourself, it helps us be more un-derstanding and compassionate for those who haven't been here long. For those who came directly from Earth, it's also customary to share your year of arrival. For you, that would be 192."

"I see. So your great grandparents were the first ones in your family to arrive," Braedon said. His expression softened. "Then you've never seen Earth. You've never felt the sun on your face."

Esmeralda's smile wilted. "A sad reality. Those of us born and raised here have only seen videos captured on phones and com-puters, like the ones you shared from your phone. We've seen it through virtual reality, but I'm sure it falls short of the real thing. It looks like such a magical place."

For the first time since arriving in Elysium, Braedon felt the pity and sorrow in which he'd been wallowing shift toward anoth-er. "I'm sorry. Hopefully someday soon they'll figure out a way to reverse the portals."

"There isn't a person in Tartarus who doesn't long for that day. But," she said, her tone changing, "until that day, we have to make the best of our lives here. Which is why I've come. Your Welcome Center team—including your doctor, psychologist, physical ther-apist, etc—have agreed you are ready for integration into society. You're being released today!"

Braedon sat up. "Took 'em long enough."

"We do apologize for that. We've learned the hard way if we release people into the population too soon, they can become a danger to others. Or themselves. The good news is you've passed all the suicide protocols."

"That's encouraging," Braedon said flatly. "So now what? You guys just drop me off on a street corner, pat me on the shoulder and say, 'Good luck, kid'?"

Esmeralda laughed. "Definitely not. Every new arrival brings with them new potential for the betterment of our society. You will be provided with an apartment rent free for the first year. And, based on your interview, we selected three career options for you to choose from." She handed him the tablet.

Braedon studied the short list: 1) Police 2) Security Guard 3) Military. He frowned as he studied the third option. "Military? Who is there to fight against?"

Her face darkened slightly. "Unfortunately, the governments of the other five cities don't always wish to cooperate. Territorial disputes have arisen, as well as…shall we say, ideological disputes."

Braedon harrumphed. "Human nature never changes, does it?" He met her gaze as he handed the tablet back. "What if I don't want any of those?"

"Then we'll do our best to accommodate your wishes. However, please understand we've had decades of experience helping new arrivals. Those who choose a career in which they're already familiar and comfortable with thrive. Others don't tend to fair so well."

He considered her statement. *She's probably right. I'm a soldier. Everything else has been taken from me. The only thing I have left is my military training.* "Fine. I'll join the military unit."

"Excellent. The Welcome Center board will be pleased," Esmeralda said. She tapped on the tablet for several moments, then looked back at him. "Let me just finish with the last of the paperwork and I'll take you to your new home."

She turned and left, leaving Braedon to his tumultuous thoughts. *New 'home'. Time to face reality, Braedon. Your life on Earth is a memory.* The thought struck him like a physical blow. *Goodbye, Cat. At least you didn't get dragged into this nightmare. I hope you find happiness.*

He stood and stepped into the bathroom. He studied his face in the mirror. "You've faced some tough challenges in your life," he said aloud. "This is no different. You can do this." After staring at his reflection a few moments longer, Braedon took in a deep breath. "Time to face the future."

True to her word, Esmeralda escorted him out of the Welcome Center less than an hour later. That first day would forever be burned in Braedon's memory. The tour of the city left him awed and amazed. The technology in Elysium was far beyond anything found on Earth in the early 21st century. The splendor of the city with its shining globe overhead almost made Braedon forget he was trapped beneath the ground.

Parks filled with trees and flowers unlike any he had ever seen were interspersed throughout the city. According to Esmeralda, they were native to Tartarus and were able to grow without sunlight. Magnificent holographic displays on the outside of buildings contrasted sharply with the natural beauty, as if in competition. The images of fantastical landscapes and creatures were so realistic, Braedon caught himself struggling to differentiate between reality and fantasy.

"What is that advertising?" Braedon asked as they passed one particular display.

"Pandora's Box," she replied. "It's virtual reality, but fully immersive. It was just launched a few months ago. Everyone *loves* it! It allows us to visit anywhere our imaginations want to go. I'll definitely take you there soon. But first you need to get acclimated to the *real* world."

After the tour, Esmeralda took Braedon to his apartment. The small studio was already furnished with the bare essentials such as a bed, table, chair, television, and couch. Dishes were also provided, and the refrigerator and cupboards were stocked with food.

They spent the next several hours shopping for clothes and other necessities. Braedon had hoped they could pick up some alcohol, but Esmeralda informed him it was strictly forbidden for new arrivals. As much as it irritated him, he had to admit it made sense. They stopped at a nearby restaurant for dinner before finally returning to Braedon's apartment.

Once all the items they had purchased were brought inside, Esmeralda turned toward the front door and gave him a warm smile. "I hope your first day in the city was a good one. Please spend the rest of the evening getting situated. I'll stop by again tomorrow to see how you're doing. You have my number if you need anything, or just want someone to talk to. If you think of something you forgot to buy, we'll go out and get it tomorrow. Just so you know, today is Friday. That gives you the weekend to settle in. On Monday, I'll take you to the military recruitment center."

"Thank you, Esmeralda. Thanks for everything."

"You're most welcome. See you tomorrow. And remember, I'm just a vid call away." With that, she winked at him and left.

4

ELYSIUM SECURITY FORCE

Braedon spent the remainder of the weekend getting his apartment in order. Esmeralda stopped in twice each day to check on him. While he appreciated her company and she was always friendly, he kept her at a distance. Not only was he still grieving the separation from Catrina, but something about Esmeralda seemed off. She was almost *too* friendly, *too* eager to help and offer assistance. Braedon told himself it was probably because most new arrivals needed the extra attention and constant care. But the cynical part of him felt there was something more hidden beneath the surface.

When the doorbell chimed at six o'clock sharp on Monday morning, Braedon was showered, dressed in his training uniform, and ready to go. He started crossing toward the door when he remembered all he had to do was give the verbal command. "Door, open."

"Good morning," Esmeralda greeted him cheerfully once the door had recessed into the wall. "Ready for your big day?"

"Every day has been a 'big day' since I arrived. I'm just looking forward to some physical activity to clear my mind."

"That's the spirit. It's important to seek out healthy activities to help you cope with the realities of your situation. Physical exercise is crucial."

"Yeah, I've heard that before. Let's just go."

They walked to Esmeralda's hovercar. Braedon still marveled how the technology embedded into the streets allowed cars to float. *So much to take in. I wonder how much soldiering has advanced. What new ways have humans devised to kill each other?*

After a short ride through the city, Esmeralda guided the vehicle toward a security checkpoint set into the road. They passed through easily and she brought the vehicle to a stop at the nearest building. They exited the car and Esmeralda led the way through the building's main entrance.

In typical military fashion, the building was sparsely decorated, focusing more on function than aesthetics. Two men with short-cropped hair were seated behind a long desk. Both were staring at the same screen with blank expressions on their faces, as if lost in a trance.

Braedon cast a concerned glance toward his guide. "What's wrong with them?" he whispered.

Esmeralda seemed unconcerned by the strange behavior. "They're communicating through their implants. Likely receiving instructions about us."

"Implants?"

His question went unanswered as the two men suddenly snapped out of their trance. The man on the right stood and came around the desk to greet them. "Esmeralda, it's good to see you again. And you must be Braedon Lewis. My name is Kyler Bough. Welcome to the ESF."

Braedon shook the offered hand.

Kyler continued. "Esmeralda sent us your file and filled us in on the circumstances of your arrival. I know it can be traumatic and disorienting, but we have to keep our eyes focused ahead. If you're looking for a shoulder to cry on, you've come to the wrong place. We'll leave that job up to your esteemed Acclamation Liaison," he finished with a wink toward Esmeralda.

"Fine by me," Braedon stated matter-of-factly. "I come from a military family, so I'm used to it. In fact, I'd be concerned if it were any different."

Kyler clapped him on the shoulder. "You oughta fit right in here. C'mon. Let me introduce you to the 'boss'." He turned his gaze toward Esmeralda. "Thanks for bringing him. We'll take it from here. And remember, you still owe me a dinner date."

She laughed lightly. "Owe you? Yeah right. After what you pulled with Sandy, the only date you'll get with me will be in the Box." She turned and gave Braedon's arm a light squeeze. "I'll be back to pick you up this afternoon. Take care."

Kyler waited for her to leave, then nodded for Braedon to follow. As they passed into an adjoining hallway, Kyler chuckled. "Watch yourself, Braedon. Esmeralda's a piece of work. One minute she's as friendly as can be, the next she'll claw your throat out."

Braedon raised an eyebrow at the comment. "Thanks. I'll keep that in mind." As they moved further down the hall, he caught sight through a doorway of a woman staring straight ahead and unmoving. She had the unsettling appearance of a life-like statue. A second later she blinked and started walking.

"Tell me about these implants. What are they? How do they work?"

A flash of hesitation crossed Kyler's face. "Over the past fifty years or so the scientists in Elysium have figured out how to create an interface between the human brain and technology. The implants allow us to do all sorts of amazing things. We can access information through the data streams just by thinking. We can link directly with devices and access their features with a thought. And we can even use them to communicate with other enhanced people without speaking."

"Enhanced?"

"Those who have technological upgrades," Kyler explained. "Those without are called 'naturals'. The procedures are quite expensive, and recoveries are rather brutal. Many purists are opposed to it on moral grounds. It has created quite a rift in our society. But the younger generation is all for it, so it won't be much longer before the enhanced are in the majority."

Braedon felt a knot form in his stomach. The idea of being able to communicate telepathically and operate machines with a thought was simultaneously exciting and terrifying. *But at what cost? What does something like that do to a person? That woman was staring blankly like a zombie!*

His thoughts were interrupted as Kyler led them through a set of double doors and into the gymnasium. Two muscular men were engaged in combat on a thick training mat in the center of the floor. A host of recruits dressed in uniforms identical to Braedon's stood in a semi-circular formation. The shorter, and younger, of the two had lighter skin and blonde hair. The taller, older man had dark skin. A black mustache and goatee outlined his mouth, which was currently pursed tightly in concentration. The ceiling lights reflected off his shaved head as he moved swiftly to counter his opponent's attacks.

Braedon watched the match with admiration. Both opponents were highly skilled in martial arts. The dark-skinned man in particular moved with a fluidity and grace Braedon had rarely seen before. The combat continued for another minute until the taller man spun and swept the feet of his opponent out from under him, sending him crashing to the mat.

The room erupted with applause. The victor reached down and helped the other to his feet, clapped him on the back, and turned to address the spectators. "Major Henly fought admirably. But maintaining your balance and footing is everything. Even the slightest misstep can mean the difference between life and death. Today we're going to focus on exactly that: creating opportunities to disrupt the balance of our opponents while maintaining our own."

The speaker caught sight of Braedon, then waved toward Major Henly and another pair of higher ranking instructors. "Take over for me."

Braedon felt the man's power and authority press upon him as he approached. Here was someone who exuded confidence and was accustomed to being obeyed. Immediately. Braedon squared his shoulders and sucked in a breath as if preparing for battle.

"Mr. Lewis, I presume," the older man said in a deep baritone voice. "I'm Master Sergeant Steven Russell, 3rd Gen."

"It's an honor to meet you, sir," Braedon responded, using his customary military bark.

Sergeant Russell smiled. "At ease, soldier. There'll be plenty of time for that later. I read in your file you're a recent arrival to our 'fair' city. You have my condolences. A transition that abrupt can have a catastrophic impact on even the most resilient and healthy minds."

"Thank you, sir," Braedon said, feeling once again the weight of recent events. "It has been difficult to adjust. I'm not one who enjoys sitting around. What I could really use right now is some activity and structure. If I can speak plainly, sir, you have incredible form and control."

"You have a trained eye," Sergeant Russell said as he nodded approvingly. "Your file says you are a second-degree black belt in Tae Kwon Do."

"Yes, sir."

"That's a good start. Are you familiar with any of the other martial arts? Jujitsu? Aikido?"

"I'm afraid not, sir."

Sergeant Russell clapped Braedon on the back. "We'll have that fixed before long. Kyler here is one of my best students. I'm going to pair you up with him."

Braedon exhaled, a smile creeping across his features. The familiarity of self-discipline served as a balm to his deep emotional wounds. Kyler pulled Braedon to a corner of the room as Sergeant Russell resumed his instruction with the remainder of the recruits.

"Okay then," Kyler said and he moved into a combat stance. "Let's start with a little sparring. Show me what you know, then I'll have a better idea of where to start."

Braedon felt his blood race with adrenaline. He dropped into his own ready stance, his arms lifted in a defense posture. He launched into a series of strikes and counterstrikes. While Kyler managed to block each attack, Braedon could tell he was caught off guard. Braedon's second attack was less successful as his opponent adjusted his fighting style to match. By the third round, Kyler began pressing his own attacks harder and harder. Although Braedon held his own, more and more of Kyler's strikes made it through his defenses.

"You've got a great foundation," Kyler said at last between heavy breaths. "You're the best new recruit we've had in a long while."

Braedon was about to respond when he caught a glimpse of

movement from one of the balcony walkways positioned along the far wall. A figure dressed in solid black, form-fitting armor looked down at him. At least, the helmeted head with its black visor was tilted at an angle consistent with a line of sight in his direction. A chill ran down Braedon's neck at the sight of the grim visage. The figure remained rooted in place for several long moments as if studying him before finally turning away and exiting through a doorway.

A shadow that had fallen over him seemed to depart as the door closed. He felt his breathing relax as if a weight compressing his chest had suddenly lifted.

"First time seeing a Guardian, huh?" Kyler asked.

Braedon tore his gaze from the balcony and turned it toward his companion. "What was that thing?"

"That was nothing more than a human with technological enhancements," Kyler said. "They're the Type I Guardians, more affectionately known as Cyborgs, for obvious reasons. They've gone beyond the typical implants. They have advanced speed and strength, as well as other technological advantages. They're the ESF's elite soldiers. Only the best and brightest are considered for the Guardian program."

"Type I? So I take it there are other types."

A slight grimace twisted Kyler's countenance. "Yeah, and trust me, you don't want one of them as an enemy. The Cyborgs are tough enough. The Type II Guardians are genetically enhanced. They're the results of the twisted imaginations of the Elysium scientists. They have genetically enhanced abilities given to them by the animal DNA spliced into their own. They aren't born. They're created in a laboratory. We call 'em Hybrids, also for obvious reasons. I've only seen one a couple of times. Take that feeling you just got a moment ago and multiply it by a hundred. They're smart, but the animal part of them makes 'em a bit unpredictable. But even they aren't as bad as the Type IIIs."

Braedon's eyes widened. "How many types are there?"

"Just the three. The IIIs combine both the technological enhancements and the genetic enhancements. Unfortunately, or maybe fortunately, there are relatively few of them who survive all the procedures. The few that do lead the rest. The Guardian program is one of the few deterrents keeping the other cities of Tartarus from attacking.

"But enough of the 'ghost stories'. Just be glad they're on our side. As long as you don't cross the Elysium government, you've got nothing to worry about. Now c'mon. Let's go another round."

Despite Kyler's assurances, Braedon couldn't shake the unsettled feeling churning in his gut. For the remainder of the day, he caught himself glancing nervously toward the balcony, expecting to see the armored figure watching him from above.

5

PANDORA'S BOX

As he had hoped, the daily routine of training gave focus and direction to Braedon's life. The days blurred together. With each passing week, he grew more and more comfortable with this new world. His friendship with both Kyler and Master Sergeant Russell grew along with his skills.

The visits from Esmeralda became infrequent. It shifted from several times a week to only once a week. Even then, the visits were short. She was pleased at his integration into the ESF and Elysium in general. Because of this, she became less and less involved in his day-to-day life.

He was, therefore, surprised when she arrived on his six-month visit with a suggestion. "You've shown amazing resilience, Braedon. You've adapted better than most. Because of that, the board has decided, based on my recommendation, to lift your restrictions."

"Restrictions? Which restrictions?"

"Alcohol, and Pandora's Box visits."

Braedon let out a sarcastic laugh. "Yay! So, I've convinced my benevolent caretakers I can be trusted not to go on a drunken virtual reality trip, huh? What an accomplishment!"

Esmeralda shifted in the chair in which she sat. "It *is* an accomplishment. Many people *never* have the restrictions lifted, especially after only six months. It takes most over a year to adapt. Some never do."

Some of Braedon's mirth deflated. "Yeah, I guess you're right. I suppose it depends on a lot of factors, such as what they left behind." His thoughts drifted toward Catrina. Yes, he missed her. But they had only been married for four rocky years and they hadn't had any children yet. He could only imagine how much harder it would've been if he had been married for decades and left small children behind who would never see their daddy again.

"Actually, not only has the board lifted the restrictions, but they're actually encouraging you to visit a Pandora's Box location. We've found the experience serves to help many feel less... trapped. New arrivals are often overwhelmed by being underground constantly. Pandora's Box makes them feel free again. It can be quite therapeutic.

"I sent coupons for four free sessions to your personal device," Esmeralda continued. "There's only one restriction: you can't visit the Earth simulations from the 21st Century. They're too close to home for you. Anything in the 20th Century or earlier is fine. And, of course, the sky's the limit when it comes to visiting other fantasy worlds and locations. Have fun! You're going to love it! And it's even more immersive if you take us up on our offer of an implant. Just think about it."

The conversation drifted to other topics. However, he couldn't stop thinking about her last statement. Since he'd first learned of the procedure, he'd given lots of thought to the idea. Esmeralda reminded him on every visit that, as a member of the ESF, the government of Elysium would pay for it.

After she left, Braedon found his thoughts constantly returning to the possibilities offered by Pandora's Box. Was it a coincidence the restrictions were dropped on a Saturday when Braedon was free and available?

Unable to resist the siren call of his own curiosity, Braedon found himself strolling through the entrance of the nearest facility later that evening.

"Welcome to Pandora's Box, where you can become God. How may I help you?" asked a beaming young woman with professionally styled short pink hair.

After pausing a moment to take in the highly polished, beautifully decorated foyer, Braedon cleared his throat and replied, "I have a seven o'clock appointment. I was told to ask for Julia."

"Sure thing. I'll get her for you," she replied. The woman's gaze became unfocused for a second before returning to normal. Braedon noticed the telltale pinprick of light on her temple indicating an implant. "She'll be here in a moment. Just have a seat in our waiting room."

He nodded politely and sat in one of the indicated chairs. However, before he had time to even settle in comfortably, a slim young woman in her late twenties came through a side door and approached him.

"Mr. Lewis, I presume," she said, her hand outstretched.

Braedon rose and shook her hand. "Hi. You must be Julia."

She smiled as she brushed a loose strand of black hair streaked with blue highlights out of her face. As she did so, Braedon noted she was also one of the "enhanced." "Come on in. We have a little paperwork to take care of, then we'll get you started on your adventure!"

He smiled hesitantly, then followed as she led him through the door, down a hallway and into a side room containing a desk and several chairs. Lining the walls of the room were screens display-ing images depicting the various possibilities awaiting him in the virtual world.

"You know, you're lucky you called when you did," she said as they entered the room. Sitting down at the desk, she pointed to-ward a chair and invited him to sit. "Normally, it can take up to two weeks to schedule an appointment, but it just so happens we had a cancellation a few minutes before you called."

"Interesting," Braedon said, his brow furrowing. *Coincidence? Or did Esmeralda pull some strings for me?* "Just out of curiosity, how come you had a cancellation? I thought that was nearly unheard of."

Julia's face darkened almost imperceptibly. "Unfortunately, one of our clients passed away unexpectedly."

Braedon's military training had included a course on reading ex-pressions. He could tell there was much more to this story than she was divulging. However, he decided not to press the topic.

"Okay. Well, I know that you're excited to get going, but there are a few things that need to be taken care of first. It'll only take about five minutes if you trust me," Julia said with a wink. "Or thirty minutes if you want to read it all for yourself." She took a tablet from the desk drawer and slid it in front of Braedon.

"This first page is a standard contract," she explained. "It outlines exactly what you can expect from your Pandora's Box experience and gives you some basic payment plan options when you choose to sign up to be a regular customer. That's after you run out of your coupons. By placing your print at the bottom, you'll get twenty percent off your entire yearly package."

When Braedon didn't respond, she changed tactics. "I tell you what, how about we skip all the talk about the package deal until after you've experienced your first session? I'm sure that once you see how amazing it is, you'll come to understand the value in what we're offering. So," she said, changing the page with a mental command via her wireless implant, "let's just jump right to the liability form."

"Liability?" Braedon said with sudden concern.

Julia gave him a wry smile. "Don't worry, it's merely a formality. This is just a way for New World Corp to cover themselves legally from those weirdos out there who are always trying to find loopholes so they can sue big companies."

"Have there ever been any cases of people getting hurt using Pandora's Box?" Braedon asked. "I thought I read something about people who—"

She interrupted him by holding up her hand. "I know what you're going to say. People are always trying to highlight odd stories or make rumors. Remember, Mr. Lewis, any time you're dealing with something that raises someone's heart rate or gets the adrenaline flowing, there's always the possibility people who aren't in the best physical shape could wind up injured. But I assure you, using Pandora's Box is no more dangerous than using exercise equipment."

His reservations still not fully placated, he nevertheless placed his thumb on the reader, giving his consent.

"Great! Now, I'm going to show you a short video explaining how to operate the program once you're hooked into the system." With another mental command, Julia activated the screen on the wall behind her and played the video.

"Welcome to Pandora's Box, where you can become God!" a narrator said. "This video will guide you through the basics of how to operate the system, as well as describe some of the many options available to you during your session." As the voiceover continued, the images on the screen changed to illustrate the various points presented.

Braedon listened intently, enraptured by the advanced technology and, at the same time, apprehensive about what it would feel like. The sensation reminded him of the first time he'd ever ridden a roller coaster.

When the video concluded, Julia finished the remainder of the paperwork, then asked Braedon to speak into a microphone in order to get a sampling of his speech patterns. She explained this would be loaded into the computer so the system would respond to his specific voice commands. Once finished, she answered a few last-minute questions, then escorted him to his private cubicle.

Butterflies performed backflips in his stomach as Braedon waited nervously for his session to begin. He now understood why it took the better part of an hour to get ready. First, the technicians had to get him into the gravity control harness, which had several small hover plates attached to it at strategic points, allowing the wearer to be fully suspended in midair. "This is so your physical movements don't interfere with the artificial sensations created by the machine," Julia had explained. Next, it took all of forty minutes for the three technicians to hook him to the machine. Finally, they activated the harness, lifting him several feet off the ground, and did several tests to make sure everything was connected properly.

Braedon stared around the small room in which he hovered. The cold gray walls gave him the uncomfortable feeling he was in some sort of cell. It was completely devoid of furniture or decorations. Even the door blended in so well with the wall it was hard to distinguish. Soft lighting was provided by two rectangular fixtures in the ceiling. And although he couldn't see it, he knew there was a camera mounted in front so the technicians could monitor him.

"Okay, Mr. Lewis. Everything's in place. Are you ready?" a male voice said.

Braedon couldn't be sure if he heard it audibly or whether it just appeared in his head. Taking a deep breath, he held it for a moment then let it out with a sigh. "I'm ready."

"Program beginning now."

The lights in the room dimmed. A screen materialized in front of him, and Braedon realized he was no longer in the harness but standing on the floor of the room. At least, that's what his senses were telling him. Lifting his feet experimentally, he gaped in awe at the realism of the sensations. Returning his gaze to the screen, he studied his options.

Main Menu
- Games
- Movies
- User Modules
- Tartarus Locations
- Earth Locations
- Historical Events
- World Creator

Remembering Julia's suggestion that he try each of them in order to understand the scope of what is offered, Braedon reached with his left hand and touched the word *Games*.

The screen changed, and a second menu appeared, listing the numerous types of available games. He selected "Mystery." He worked through a few more menus to customize his game, then pressed the final button to launch the program.

The room around him dissolved. Braedon watched in amazement as his surroundings changed. He was standing on a dark street corner at night in what looked to be a small town on Earth sometime in the 1930s. A solitary streetlight shone down upon him.

Despite the incredible changes in his surroundings, Braedon couldn't help but look up. Instead of seeing a rock ceiling, there was nothing but open space and stars! Tears welled in his eyes as the memories of Earth washed over him. Overwhelmed, he leaned against a storefront window and regained his composure.

He caught sight of his reflection in the glass. The face staring back at him wasn't his own, but that of a strikingly handsome man in his late twenties dressed in a pinstriped business suit, trench coat, and fedora.

He reached out and touched the glass. He was surprised at how real it felt. He moved his hand along it, then felt the brick wall, the door, and even the handle. Despite the realistic feel of the virtual world, it still wasn't quite as natural as Braedon had expected. The more he studied it, the more he realized things didn't quite match reality. "Man can do some amazing things, but he still can't quite compete with Mother Nature," he said aloud.

From somewhere behind him he heard a woman scream. He turned and ran down the street toward the sound. He rounded a corner to find an elegantly dressed woman slumped against a wall. She wore a beautiful red business suit, and her head was covered with a white hat with red trim.

"What's wrong, ma'am?" Braedon asked in concern.

When she looked up at him, Braedon felt his pulse quicken. She moved with a fluidity that was too smooth—the kind of movement only a computer could generate. But Braedon barely noticed due to the incredible beauty of the woman. Her full red lips stood out in stark contrast to her porcelain face. As he stood dumbstruck, she held out a white-gloved, delicate hand. Braedon took hold of it and pulled her to her feet.

"Thank you, sir," she replied softly. "It was horrible! I was just locking up my shop for the night and heading for home when… when it appeared!"

"What appeared?" Braedon asked.

"A figure, cloaked in black," she answered, holding his arm tightly.

Although still aware he was inside a virtual world, he was shocked at how the programmers had managed to fool the senses. The woman's hand on his arm felt real. He could hear sounds all around him, and even smell the woman's perfume.

An uncomfortable sense of shame washed over him as his wife's image appeared in his mind. *C'mon, Braedon, you don't have to feel ashamed of being attracted to a woman in a virtual world. It's not like it's real.* Even as the thought crossed his mind, another one followed. *But isn't being unfaithful to your wife in your mind just as bad as being unfaithful to her physically? In many ways, isn't it worse?* Braedon pushed the thoughts away and focused on the story in which he now played a role.

"If you don't mind, sir, would you please walk me to my car?" the woman asked.

Braedon listened as she told him more about the mysterious figure. However, once they reached her car, she stumbled and collapsed in his arms. He was startled to find she was unconscious. He set her gently to the ground and tried to revive her. Police sirens rent the air and were growing louder with each passing second.

Before he knew it, he was surrounded by officers, their weapons trained on him. "Don't move!" one of them commanded. "Step away from the woman!"

Braedon raised his hands over his head and complied with the order as another officer checked the woman's pulse. "She's dead!" he announced.

Although Braedon was interested in this new twist to the plot of the game, he was also keenly aware his time in Pandora's Box would be over soon enough. He still had other menu options to explore.

"Return to the Main Menu," he said loudly. The scene around him froze before dissolving. A moment later he was back where he started, the menu screen hovering in front of him. This time he selected the movie option. The screen changed to show several search criteria. Braedon browsed through the available movies. Esmeralda's words echoed in his mind as his eyes landed on one particular title.

"The sky's the limit when it comes to visiting other fantasy worlds and locations."

He smiled and selected *The Lion, the Witch, and the Wardrobe* from the *Chronicles of Narnia* film series. To his delight, he found he could select either to enter the movie as an observer or choose which character he would like to portray in the film. He selected the former. Instead of starting at the beginning of the film, he chose to observe the final battle sequence. The room dimmed as the movie started.

Although this film series had been one of his favorites as a child and he had seen it numerous times over the years, he had never experienced it like this. Instead of being limited to the perspective of the camera, Braedon now found himself *in* the battle! Fauns, centaurs, minotaurs, and other fantastic creatures fought mere feet away from where he stood in the center of the battlefield. Behind him on the grassy hills were the archers, while in front of him, Peter Pevensie, dressed in full battle armor, dueled with the evil White Witch, Jadis.

A leopard and panther were locked in battle and nearly fell into him, causing Braedon to leap to the side to avoid being struck. As he did so, he noticed he was wearing his regular clothing. He realized through trial and error that although he was inside the movie, he could not affect the movie. As the menu had stated, he was merely an observer.

He watched the battle from various vantage points, each time focusing on a different character or action sequence. Several times he commanded the computer to rewind the scene so he could watch it from a different perspective. After about ten minutes, he decided to try the second option from the submenu. He gave the command to the computer and waited. The action around him froze, then changed to match his new request.

Braedon smiled broadly as the scenery around him took shape. All the excitement he had felt as a child came rushing back. He always wanted to be King Peter, and now, thanks to Pandora's Box, he *was* King Peter! Looking down at his body, he saw he was dressed in the full battle armor of Peter Pevensie, including a sword and shield.

The White Witch leapt toward him, her sword blades whirling in slow motion. It was then he remembered the words from the Pandora's Box instruction video.

"When you take on the role of a character, it becomes more of a video game. You have to act out the part—speak the lines, do the actions of the character, etc. The program will guide you by showing you what lines to say or what actions to take. Once you get the hang of it, you can even adjust the speed of the movie so the action sequences come at you faster. Just follow along and have fun!"

As the witch's blades drew near, a red arrow a foot long appeared in front of him, pointing down. Braedon followed its instructions and ducked. The swords flew over his head. Another arrow appeared on his sword and showed a thrusting maneuver. Braedon again followed the arrow's lead and thrust his sword at his enemy.

He continued to follow the motions, completing the action sequence. When the initial novelty of the technology had worn off, Braedon decided to see just what the limitations were. Rewinding the scene, he started it over. Instead of fighting the queen, he turned and tried running away. But no matter how much he ran, his surroundings never changed. Disappointed, he tried another tactic. When the White Witch attacked, he just stood there and let her swords slice at him. Once again, though, he found his actions caused the film to freeze. Finally deciding to have one last bit of fun with the machine, he leaned in toward the frozen image of the fierce woman, stuck out his tongue, and blew raspberries at her. Laughing out loud, he took his sword and threw it into the air where it disappeared, only to reappear in the sheath at his side.

This is fantastic! he thought. *I could spend hours in here.*

The thought sobered him immediately. *That's exactly what has happened to others. Now I see why people can easily get addicted.* "Return to the Main Menu," he said aloud, his thoughts still wrestling with the implications of his experiences in the virtual world.

Back at the Main Menu, Braedon decided to skip over the User Modules, which according to the instruction video, were "Those invented by our other clients," and chose "Earth Locations" instead. Tears began to pool in his eyes as he studied the submenu. Most of the major cities across the globe such as Paris, London, New York, Hong Kong, and Jerusalem were listed, as well as sites like the Grand Canyon, the Great Wall of China, and Niagara Falls. In a daze, Braedon accessed the program for Paris and made a specific selection on the map of the city. The menu disappeared and Braedon found himself staring at a digital rendition of the Eiffel Tower.

As he stood in the plaza, the virtual world seemed to fade. Braedon found himself caught in his own memories. He remembered walking beneath the tower, holding hands with Catrina as they took in the sights. He knew he could spend hours visiting the different locations available in the program. Yet he also knew each would only serve to increase his longing to return to Earth. *Esmeralda was right. This is too painful. I'm not ready for this.* "Return to the Main Menu," he commanded aloud.

Having become familiar with the workings of the program, Braedon spent only a moment selecting the "Historical Events" feature. He read through the list of possible choices, trying to decide which to visit. With his thoughts still dwelling on his wife, he chose an event she would have been interested in—the Crucifixion of Jesus.

The scenery around him changed to show the ancient city of Jerusalem. Again, Braedon found the computer imagery, as amazing as it was, still had a fake quality to it. He was standing in a courtyard filled with an angry crowd. Similar to the movie program, he quickly discovered he was only a spectator, not a participant in the program.

Pontius Pilate, the Roman prefect, looked down upon the crowd. A bruised and battered man wearing a purple robe and white loincloth stood next to him. Pontius Pilate quieted the crowd as Braedon climbed the steps toward the men in order to get a better view. The Jesus standing before him looked like someone from a Hollywood movie. He was handsome, and although he was bruised and beaten, the blood running down his computer-generated abdomen looked thin and unrealistic.

"Are you the Son of God?" Pilate asked Jesus in a loud voice so the crowd could hear. Jesus shook his head and looked directly at the people. "I am *a* Son of God. The kingdom of heaven is within each of us."

Braedon frowned at the words. He wouldn't have called himself versed in the Bible, despite attending church numerous times in the past. But Catrina knew it quite well. In fact, he remembered an argument they had had about this very topic. He didn't remember what the Bible recorded, but he was sure this wasn't it. The makers of Pandora's Box had obviously not done their homework. *Unless they did this deliberately.*

An idea struck him, causing his stomach to turn. He remembered the articles he had read about how the government was investing money to buy scaled-down versions of Pandora's Box for the public school system. *This virtual world, this machine, is being used to educate. With it, the programmers can change history, and because it's presented in such a powerful way, the masses will believe it unquestioningly. They're rewriting history to suit their own agendas. What other changes have they made?*

I guess like every other tool, it's a matter of who's using it. If used properly, this machine could be an incredible teaching tool. But if misused, it could become a device used for brainwashing. And if combined with the other entertainment features, a tool to promote all kinds of social evils and perverse behaviors.

Still mulling over his disturbing thoughts, Braedon returned to the Main Menu and chose the final selection, "World Creator." He worked through several more menus in order to set the parameters of his new world. When he finished, the program started. He found himself standing in a wide-open field on Earth that stretched to the horizon in every direction. He followed the instructions given in the video prior to his session and said, "Create mountains." A screen appeared before him showing several types of mountain ranges. "Selection E, placement fifty miles from center. Size: seventy percent." A moment later, snow-capped mountains appeared to his right. "Reduce height to sixty percent," Braedon said. The height of the mountains shrunk slightly.

Awed by the sheer possibilities of what he could accomplish, he continued with renewed vigor. "Create river." Again, the screen appeared, showing various river choices. "Selection J, placement fifteen miles from center. Length: twenty miles north and ten miles south from center."

Braedon lost track of time as he became immersed in the creation of his world. He was therefore shocked when his handiwork dissolved and the plain nondescript room came back into focus. After two hours in the virtual world, it took Braedon several seconds to remember where he was and why he was in a harness hanging several feet off the floor.

The technicians entered, unhooked him, and helped him regain his balance. Julia met him as he exited the room, his mind still reeling from all he had experienced. "Well, what did you think? Didn't I tell you it was amazing?"

"Yes," Braedon responded dumbly, "one could get lost in there."

Although he didn't intend it as a compliment, she took the comment and ran with it. "I know, right? One time, I did get lost in my own created world. But rather than just jump back to the main menu, I explored for a while and made a game out of finding my way back to the mansion I created. And time seems to pass so quickly, doesn't it?"

"Yeah," was all Braedon could manage.

"So why don't you come in here to my office and let's talk about our packages?"

An hour later, Braedon left Pandora's Box with a two-year session agreement. Despite his misgivings and uncertainty, his desire to return to the virtual world overrode any concerns. His return drive in his new hovercar was a blur. The excitement of his recent experience and his tumultuous thoughts about the uses of the technology consumed him. He entered his apartment and immediately activated his phone. When the voice on the other side picked up, he said, "Hi. This is Braedon Lewis. I'm a member of the ESF. I'd like to schedule an appointment to receive a wireless implant."

6

CONSPIRACIES

"Well, buddy, here's to the completion of your first year of training with the ESF," Kyler said, lifting his glass.

Braedon raised his own and clinked it against Kyler's before taking a drink. "Thanks, I guess."

"Whatdya mean, 'I guess'? You're flying through the classes. At the pace you're going, you'll be in active duty in another six months. Master Sergeant Russell is very impressed with your previous training."

"Speaking of the old man, I thought you said he was going to join us," Braedon commented as he glanced around the restaurant once more.

Kyler shrugged. "Who knows? Maybe something came up with his wife and kids. When you're married, you can't just come and go as you please. You've always got to check with your wife first."

Braedon felt the familiar emptiness settle on him. *Yeah, I remember. But I'd give anything to have my wife by my side again.* Not wanting to sour the mood, he turned the conversation back on his friend. "Ha! Listen to you. You act as if being married is a bad thing, yet the way things are going with Eliana, you'll be joining the ranks of the committed before I become a member of the ESF!"

Kyler smiled wryly. "I never said it was a *bad* thing to have to check with your girl first. I was just making a general statement."

"Right!" Braedon laughed.

As the evening wore on, the pair was joined by several other recruits. Braedon enjoyed their camaraderie, yet with each passing minute his concern for his teacher grew. One of the advantages of his new implant was he could contact anyone with a mere thought. He reached out to Steven on multiple occasions as the night wore on, but received no response. The silence was uncharacteristic for the strict disciplinarian.

By eight o'clock, Kyler said his goodbyes and left Braedon in the company of the others. Another hour passed before Braedon finally left the restaurant for home. The Globe had dimmed to its 'moon' setting and was now making its way back across the roof of the massive cavern.

Braedon, I need to talk to you.

He heard Steven's voice through his implant. Although the message wasn't audible, the technicians made recordings of each person's voice and programmed the implants so others would hear the messages in the voice of the sender.

It's good to hear from you, Braedon replied. *I was beginning to worry. Is everything okay? What's going on?*

I'll tell you in person. I'm waiting for you at your apartment.

I'm almost there. See you in a few.

The connection severed. Braedon's unease grew. Something was *definitely* wrong.

He pulled into the parking lot near his apartment and exited the car. The 'moonlight' from the Globe shown down on Steven's frame as he stood near the entrance of the apartment complex. Braedon opened the door and gestured for his instructor to enter. Once they were inside the apartment and the door had closed behind them, he turned toward Steven. "You don't look so good. What's going on?"

Steven stroked his goatee and began pacing the room. Braedon noticed the unusual slump in his teacher's shoulders. When he spoke, his voice was low and reserved.

"Braedon, I want you to know you're one of my most gifted students. Since the moment you entered my training facility, I've been impressed by not only your skills, but also your character. You've come a long way in the past year.""Thank you, Master Sergeant Russell," Braedon said cautiously, wondering at the strange start to the conversation.

"Please, call me Steven."

Braedon frowned. "I'm not sure I'm comfortable with that, sir. Protocol dictates—"

"Protocol no longer applies. As of today, I am no longer a part of the Elysium Security Forces."

"What?" Braedon gasped. "That's insane! What happened?"

"Braedon, do you trust me?"

"Yes," he replied without hesitation. "I trust you with my life. You're one of the most respectable men I've ever known."

Steven was silent for a moment before responding. "Interesting choice of words. If that's the case, then I need you to trust me now. What I'm about to say is going to be difficult to hear."

Braedon inhaled slowly. "Okay. I'm with you. What's going on?"

The dark-skinned man settled his large frame into a recliner and motioned to the couch. Braedon sat down, his eyes never leaving his mentor. Once they were settled in, Steven began.

"As you know, Governor Devyn Mathison is a shrewd man. His father was the governor of Elysium during the War of 163. At the time, Devyn was a lawyer. But after his father and brother were assassinated by Jihadists, he turned to politics. He had a long career as a council member before finally being elected governor a few years ago. Since taking office, he has put a lot of emphasis on the Guardian program, as well as passing a slew of...shall we say... restrictive laws."

"Yeah, I've gathered that," Braedon said. "Just in the past year I've noticed some changes."

"Exactly. But for someone like me who has been born and raised in Elysium, the changes have been even more dramatic. Over the past two years, many of us who are concerned about his governmental overreach have banded together and started speaking out, mostly through anonymous methods. We've started an organization called Crimson Liberty."

Braedon's eyes widened. "What? *You're* one of the founding members? I've heard rumors about that group—and none of them positive."

"Of course not. Mathison doesn't like when people challenge his policies," Steven said with a smirk. "And that brings us to the present situation. Mathison's spies have finally connected the dots."

"They know you're a leader in Crimson Liberty," Braedon said numbly.

Steven nodded. "And now they're doing everything in their power to take me down. Listen, Braedon. Devyn Mathison has more power than probably anyone in Tartarus, and his power grows every day. Even more than that, he's willing to do anything to secure that power. He's on a 'righteous crusade' to cleanse Tartarus of those who oppose him. Now that he knows the truth about me, my life is in danger."

Braedon shook his head. "No way. If he lays a finger on you, more than half of the ESF will turn on him! The men are loyal to you, sir. Say the word and we'll remove him forcibly from office!"

Steven let out a heavy sigh. "He knows that. Which is why he won't kill me. He'll discredit me."

"Discredit you? How?"

"As I said, Mathison is shrewd. If he kills me, he makes me a martyr. He knows the men are loyal. So he…"

A flood of message notifications came through Braedon's implant simultaneously. One of them was an emergency notification from the Elysium government.

"Time's up," Steven said heavily. "Go ahead. Access the feed so you can hear the lies firsthand."

Braedon's stomach churned as he sent the command through his implant. The screen on the wall flickered to life. A reporter was speaking into the camera.

"…evidence has come to light implicating one of the top military trainers, Master Sergeant Steven Russell. In recent years, a new anti-government organization known as Crimson Liberty has been spreading disinformation and propaganda through various outlets. This group is known for its cultic beliefs and religious rhetoric. We have now learned that Steven Russell has not only been linked to the group, but is one of their founding members and chief proponents."

The scene switched to the image of the sharply dressed governor. "This is a sad day for our fair city. It appears one of our most trusted military instructors has been living a double life. By day he trains the future soldiers of the ESF. But after hours he seeks to subvert the fairly-elected officials and government he claims to defend. It grieves me to know the betrayal goes even deeper than his anti-government efforts. It goes to the heart of his own personal life."

Braedon glanced toward Steven in shock, his heart pounding in his chest. He returned his gaze to the screen as the commentator continued. "Our reporters have confirmed that Steven Russell, husband, father, and grand-father, has been carrying on secret affairs with numerous women for the past eight years. At least one woman has come forward with testimony that has been verified with hundreds of private messages and e-mails. Bank records show Mr. Russell has paid thousands of dollars over the years for 'unspecified services'. And, as of today, he has withdrawn nearly all the funds from the joint account with his beloved wife, leaving her penniless and destitute.

"When confronted with these allegations, Russell immediately resigned from the Elysium Security Forces and, despite our many efforts to reach him, has declined an interview. Sadly, this isn't the first time Tamera Russell has faced betrayal. Jonathan Cooney is here with more on that side of the story."

Braedon turned off the feed. A melancholy silence hung in the air. When Steven finally spoke, his voice was heavy with grief. "Tamera won't speak to me. My sons won't respond to my messages."

"They believe it's true," Braedon breathed in acknowledgment. "But how could they? They know you!"

"The strongest lies are those based on the truth," Steven said. "Early in our marriage, before I became a Christian, I cheated on Tamera. In fact, it was that failure that brought me to faith. We worked through it and came out stronger. But Mathison must have found out about it. He played off my wife's past fears. And, with his power and connections, he was able to create false evidence strong enough to stand up in a court, which he no doubt also controls. I'm ruined."

Braedon remained silent for several heartbeats. "So why are you here?" he said at last. "Why did you come to me?"

"I already spoke with Kyler after he left the restaurant and filled him in. With his seniority, he'll likely take over my position. Mathison has won this round and dealt a severe blow to Crimson Liberty. If we're going to survive and have any chance of stopping his power grab, we need more help. We need people in key positions. The other recruits look up to you. Between you and Kyler, you could work on the inside and gather intel."

Braedon took in a breath to speak, but Steven cut him off. "Before you say anything, I want you to know I completely understand the position I'm putting you in right now. How can I expect you to believe me when my own family is convinced the allegations are true? I'm not asking for a definitive answer at this time. Just let me share with you some of the info and evidence Crimson Liberty has uncovered. When you learn the truth about what Mathison is doing, you'll see why he's attacking me. Again, I'm taking a huge risk just talking to you and Kyler. If either of you turn on me, it could destroy everything we've worked to achieve. But I'm convinced, based on your character, you'll see through the lies."

Steven stood, crossed over and placed a hand on Braedon's shoulder. "I'll send you the information. Take your time. Read it over and think about it. Then get back to me with your answer. Take care, my friend. I'll be praying for you."

Overwhelmed, Braedon didn't respond. His eyes followed his friend and mentor as he left the apartment. Braedon let his head fall into his open palms. *What if it's true? If Steven is right, then I've not only been ripped from my life on Earth to be trapped in an underground world, I'm now working for a power-hungry dictator who's willing to destroy a man's life and career to eliminate any opposition to his rule. And if I join Steven, I'll become a spy against my own government with a target on my back!*

7

CROSSROADS

The day Braedon knew was coming, and had dreaded, finally arrived.

"Mr. Lewis, General Wells will see you now."

Braedon stood and straightened his uniform. It wouldn't be proper to appear before a general with wrinkles. He squared his shoulders and strode through the door into the general's office. He paused in the doorway and saluted.

Although he was in his mid-fifties, General Wells was in excellent physical condition. He returned the salute, then relaxed his posture. "At ease, Sergeant Lewis. Please, have a seat."

Braedon sat in one of the plush chairs in front of the general's desk. He fought against his bad habit of letting his leg bounce when he was nervous. He took several deep breaths to calm his nerves.

"Sergeant, your record is impeccable. Since joining the ESF six years ago, you have demonstrated superior skills and proven to have a keen intelligence. You think quickly on your feet and have excelled in all tasks assigned to you."

Sweat trickled down the back of Braedon's neck and into his collar. *Here it comes. God, help me.*

"Though we are currently at peace, threats to our beautiful city are ever present," the general began. "We have to be prepared for the future. Our intel indicates the size of the military in the other five cities has been increasing steadily over the past ten years. The numbers in Dehali and Bab al-Jihad are especially concerning. We cannot afford to be slack in our duty to defend Elysium.

"This is precisely why we pushed our scientists to develop the Guardian program. They represent our best and brightest. They are our strongest and most elite troops. Because of this, we only invite our top recruits to join their ranks.

"That is why we want you, Sergeant Lewis, to become a Guardian! We need you to secure our future!"

Braedon swallowed to clear the lump out of his throat. He knew what he had to say. He and Steven had talked about it many times. His mind drifted back to their last conversation.

"Braedon, we were wrong," Steven said, grief in his eyes. "Kyler is...he's lost to us."

"What? What do you mean, lost?" Braedon asked.

"He joined the Guardian program."

Braedon felt his skin grow cold at the news.

Steven continued. "He and I decided we needed someone on the inside to feed us information about what the program was really trying to accomplish. He volunteered. But...I saw the negative changes almost immediately. He became distant...closed off. He seemed to lose interest in everything else. His mind was focused solely on becoming a full Guardian. Even Eliana noticed the difference. She said he seemed to be in his own world most of the time. He never wants to spend time with her anymore.

"And...the surgeries took their toll on him. The plan for him was to drop out of the program if it became too much to handle. But we didn't count on them getting so deep into his head. They brainwashed him. I don't know what else to call it. The man we knew *and loved is gone. We used to jokingly call the Type I Guardians 'Cyborgs'. We didn't realize how fitting the name truly was. When Mathison's people started the program years ago, the men who joined maintained their personalities. But things have progressed far more quickly than we had anticipated.*

"No matter the consequences, when the day comes, you must refuse their request. You must not become a Guardian!"

"Sergeant Lewis?"

Braedon snapped back to the present. He breathed deeply and straightened his posture. "This is a great honor, sir. I'm overwhelmed by the responsibility."

The general smiled broadly. "Well stated. We look forward to having you among the ranks of the elite. I'll notify the commander to expect you first thing on Monday."

Braedon stood. "You misunderstand, sir. While it *is* a great honor, I must respectfully decline."

General Wells frowned. "Explain."

"Sir, I want to do everything I can to protect the innocent. However, I am simply not comfortable with the procedures required to become a Guardian."

The general's frown softened. "Many say that. But I assure you, they're completely harmless. They're simply designed to enhance your strength and speed. And, if at any point, you don't wish to proceed, you can drop out of the program."

Braedon fought against the sneer threatening to reveal itself. *Right. I'm sure that's what you told Kyler. But you fail to mention you alter the brain in such a way the victim loses the* will *to drop out.*

"Why don't you just start the program and see what you think," the general said warmly. "You're the perfect candidate. Your Acclimation Liaison indicated in her report you had no moral qualms about receiving the implant, so you aren't opposed to the technology. And she indicated you have no addictions to alcohol, drugs, or Pandora's Box. So then, what's the problem?"

There it was. The truth struck Braedon like a physical blow. The implants were the first step. The technology hit the general market around the same time the Guardian program was launched. The implants were likely a way for the government to get the average citizen to accept the idea of enhancement. That was why Esmeralda pushed him to try Pandora's Box. She was pushing him toward the implant.

He *was* the perfect candidate for the Guardian program. He was 1st Generation, only recently arrived from Earth. He was single and had no family. He was an excellent soldier. No one would miss him. He could become a robot whose sole purpose in life was to fight to preserve Elysium.

Braedon swallowed hard. "I'm sorry, sir. I cannot accept this assignment."

General Wells furrowed his brow, his posture stiffening. "Well, then. I am truly sorry to hear that. You place me in a difficult position. We need everyone in our leadership to be team players. If you're unwilling to step into that role, then I'm afraid you won't be able to advance any further. We place a high value on an individual's right to follow his or her conscience. I respect you for that. But I must also take this into consideration when choosing your next assignment. You are dismissed."

Braedon arrived at the secret Crimson Liberty safe house and tapped on the door using the specific rhythmic code. The door opened a moment later, allowing him entrance.

"I didn't expect you today," Steven said in greeting. A young man with skin nearly as dark as Steven's stood next to him. "You remember Jace, right?"

"Yeah," Braedon shook the young man's hand. "You're one of the new recruits, right?"

"Yep," Jace replied. "I've only been in the program for six months. But I've already seen enough to know I don't like the direction things are going."

"And it's only getting worse."

"What's wrong?" Steven asked. "Is everything okay?"

Braedon shook his head and settled into one of the chairs. "General Wells asked me to join the Guardian program."

Steven let out a heavy sigh as he and Jace sat on the couch across from him. "You declined, right?"

Braedon nodded. "Are you kidding? After what happened to Kyler? I was just hoping I'd be able to stay in my current position for longer. This is going to limit our intel unless one of our other agents can achieve higher rank."

Steven glanced at Jace. "Fortunately, we have others already working their way up the ladder. But we might need to instruct them not to excel quite so much. If the ESF leadership is recruiting their top soldiers for the Guardian program, then we need our people to not strive for those top positions."

"Exactly," Braedon agreed. "But I think I just figured out another piece of the puzzle. General Wells referenced the report from my Acclimation Liaison, Esmeralda. In it she noted I had 'no moral qualms about receiving the implant'. The ESF brass are clearly targeting those soldiers who are open to enhancement. It got me wondering whether or not Pandora's Box was designed to get the citizens of Elysium to be open to the concept."

Steven frowned. "That's a frightening conclusion. If the government's behind the Pandora's Box corporation, who knows what else they have planned. We'll have to get some of our agents to look into it. Maybe you can do some poking around on the side while you still have access to the…" His voice trailed off as he noticed the look on Braedon's face. "What?"

"It's too late for that. I got a message through my implant before I arrived that I'd already been reassigned."

"That quickly, huh? They must have guessed your response and had another post in mind. What's the new assignment?"

"I've been demoted. They're sending me to be a night guard at the Research and Records Compound."

Jace winced. "Yikes. That's quite a demotion.

"I guess they don't appreciate being told 'no'," Steven said wryly. "Do you think they suspect you're involved with Crimson Liberty?"

"Maybe. They know you trained me my first year in the academy."

His mentor bowed his head and closed his eyes momentarily. When he looked up again, his expression was one of resolve and confidence. "My friend, you are still young in your faith. We must have faith God is guiding our path. Do you think this caught him by surprise? Our job is to be faithful and do everything we can to walk uprightly. The results are up to him."

Braedon let out a heavy sigh. "I understand. It's just…what good am I going to be as a night guard?"

"I don't know," Steven said. "Continue to do your job to the best of your ability and look for opportunities. But always be ready. You never know when the time will come for you to act."

8

OPPORTUNITIES

Braedon massaged the muscles in his left shoulder with his right hand as he passed through the security checkpoint of the Research and Records compound. He let out a heavy sigh. *Here we go again. Another boring night. Mathison's government is getting more restrictive every day, and I'm helpless to do anything about it!* He paused and offered up a brief prayer to overcome his frustration.

He had been at his new post for almost four years. Despite Steven's encouragement, this job afforded him no opportunities to provide intel to Crimson Liberty. *How long, Lord? The ESF has already compromised several of our safe houses. They're getting close to shutting us down. And while others are dying and running for their lives, I'm here baby-sitting the very computers with the information we need. But I can't access them! If something doesn't change soon, I don't think we're going to be able to last much longer.*

"Hey, Lewis. Did you watch the game yesterday?"

Braedon turned toward one of the two guards manning the checkpoint. Despite his turbulent thoughts, he forced himself to engage in the small talk. "Yeah. That Teschler is a beast!"

"I'll say. Three goals and five saves! Just amazing. Riggs, did you see it."

"Naw," the other guard replied. "I was out with my girlfriend last night. I caught bits and pieces on the screens."

Braedon took advantage of the fact that Walker's focus had switched to Riggs and slipped down the hall. He arrived in the employee ready room to find the other night guard, Nick, ready and waiting. The two of them had shared this menial duty so many times over the past several years, Nick barely acknowledged Braedon's presence with a glance and slight nod.

Braedon stepped to his locker and grabbed his gear. He used his implant to pull up the evening's duty schedule while putting on his dark-gray guard's jacket and matching hat. "Looks like Captain Hubing assigned you to the east and south wings again," Braedon commented.

"Surprise, surprise. Same stuff, different day." With that, Nick grabbed his weapon, slipped it into the holster on his hip, and left the room.

The first few hours passed uneventfully, leaving Braedon alone with his thoughts as he patrolled the facility. As night was settling in, a message from the captain came through his implant.

Lewis, Szulcewski, we've picked up an anomaly. The techs have detected a signal floating around in the compound. It's strongest near Research Lab 118, south wing C. I need the two of you to check it out. One of the idiot researchers probably forgot to shut down his terminal again.

We're on it, Braedon replied. *Nick, I'll meet you at the north end of the hallway.*

Confirmed.

Braedon headed toward the south wing, thankful for something to do. Nick arrived at the meeting place a minute later.

"Hey, some 'excitement' for once."

Braedon snickered. "Right. Someone's head's gonna roll if it turns out to be another false…" His voice trailed off as he noticed a few rays of light peeping out from under a pair of doors at the end of the hallway. "That's odd."

"What is?" Nick said, his gaze following Braedon's.

"Is anyone scheduled to be working late in the Research Lab?"

"Not that I know of."

"There's a light on."

"Don't get your hopes up. Those motion sensors get tripped by accident all the time."

Braedon shrugged. "Maybe. But two anomalies in the same location?" His hand drifted down to rest on the hilt of his gun as they reached the door. He pressed his thumb to the plate on the wall and the doors opened.

His eyes scanned the large room searching for anything out of the ordinary. Several tables surrounded by stools rested in the center of the floor and along the walls. Above the workstations were cabinets and shelves containing various items, books, and other materials. Two doors on opposite sides of the lab lead to storage rooms. Nearly the entire length of the wall opposite the door consisted of several large windows made of thick glass looking into an adjoining area. Inside was an object that appeared to be some kind of weapon.

Braedon relaxed and let out a sigh. Everything was exactly as it should be.

"See? I told you," Nick said. "Stupid motion sensors."

Braedon strode toward a workstation on the left. "I'll check these. Take a look at the row on the other side." He examined each of the computers for any signs of activity. Sure enough, the third one on the end revealed a tiny pinprick of light, indicating the power was on. "Found it," he called out. "Yep. Someone forgot to shut down their workstation again." He flicked the power switch and the light flickered off.

As he and Nick headed toward the exit, Braedon felt something nagging at the edge of his mind. Something about the entire situation unsettled him. Nick remained silent as they walked down the hall, no doubt using his implant to communicate with the captain.

An image suddenly flashed across his mind. He stopped mid-stride in shock. *There was a data stick in the port! What if...what if someone had been in the lab and was downloading something? But they would've been seen by the cameras, unless... That anomaly! It wasn't from the computer. It was from someone in security covering their tracks. But if they're willing to risk so much, then whatever data they were stealing must be highly valuable! I've got to find a way to connect with them.*

A message came through his implant from Captain Hubing, interrupting his thoughts. *I need you to head back to that lab.*

Nick exchanged a puzzled glance with Braedon before responding. *Why, sir? The lab is empty.*

We just discovered the signal was encrypted, and it didn't go away when Braedon shut down the computer. We've blocked it now. When you were in the lab, did you check the storage rooms?

No, sir, Braedon replied, his heart pounding.

The captain swore. *We may have a security breach. The camera feeds in that area are scrambled. Go back and check every nook and cranny.*

On our way! Nick said. He motioned toward Braedon, and together they sprinted back down the hallway.

They burst through the double doors, laser pistols drawn and ready. Standing next to the workstation Braedon had examined was an elderly man dressed in a white lab coat. His hands shot into the air in fright. At his feet was a large cloth carry bag.

"Freeze!" Braedon commanded. He lifted his gun and pointed it at the intruder. "Nick, check the closets."

While his partner searched the room, Braedon drew nearer to his captive. He looked to be in his late fifties or early sixties. His hair was gray and receding. His slightly overweight body was outfitted in a dress shirt and pants beneath the white lab coat.

Braedon's mind was a flurry of activity as he considered his options. *Do I help him? If I do, I'll blow my cover for sure. But it might be worth it. I've got to find out what he was after!*

Nick finished his search. "It looks like he's alone." He came up behind the intruder and handcuffed him. The old man fell to his knees, his expression one of resignation and fear.

With his partner distracted, Braedon casually crossed to the computer, withdrew the data stick, and placed it in the pocket of his shirt.

Nick's expression had gone blank again as he communicated with the captain. Braedon reached down and opened the bag resting on the floor.

"What's in the satchel?" Nick asked.

Braedon sucked in a breath. He stood and glanced through the nearby window into the adjoining room. "It's the weapon that was in there," he replied, forcing his voice to remain calm as a new idea wormed its way into his mind. "Go see if anything else is missing."

Nick nodded and headed into the other room. Now that he was alone with the intruder, Braedon turned his full attention to the man. "What is this weapon? What were you after?"

The elderly man looked up at Braedon, his expression one of desperation. "Please, you don't understand. Mathison's people took my research and used it to create this weapon. But with it I can...I can reverse the portals! I can get us back to earth!"

9

ESCAPING THE COMPOUND

This is it! This is the moment I've been waiting for!

Years of working beneath the government's radar forced him to take a moment to check his excitement. *Hold on. Think this through. If you get this wrong, you'll lose everything. First of all, do I believe this stranger? Can I trust him?* He replayed the last few minutes in his mind. *The only way he could've gotten this far undetected by security is if he had help. If someone's helping him, then others believe him enough to place their lives on the line. Unless this is some elaborate ruse to test my loyalty. Maybe someone suspects I work for Crimson Liberty and is trying… No, that can't be it. That's real terror in his eyes.*

Nick emerged from the other room and crossed to stand beside Braedon. His presence was like a bucket of cold water thrown in Braedon's face.

"It looks like he only took the weapon," Nick said. "Nothing else appears missing. But we'll need to search him to make sure." He took a step toward the intruder. "I don't know who you are, but you picked the wrong night to break in, grandpa."

This was Braedon's chance. Captain Hubing said the camera feeds were scrambled. They wouldn't know what happened. Nick's back was facing him. He had mere seconds to make a decision.

In one fluid motion, Braedon withdrew his pistol, set it to stun, and shot Nick in the back. His unconscious form fell backward onto the old man. Braedon quickly holstered his weapon and dove forward. He helped the startled man push Nick aside and lay him on the floor.

"I need you to do exactly as I say if you want to live," Braedon said. "There's no time for questions. Do you understand?"

The old man stared blankly for several seconds as if his mind was struggling to process what was happening. Braedon pulled him to his feet and removed the bindings from his wrists.

Lewis, Szulcewski, report. We detected weapons fire from your position.

Braedon turned his attention inward to reply to his captain. *Everything's under control. The intruder tried to take my gun. But I stunned the idiot.*

Good. We'll definitely need him for questioning. Take him to head-quarters. They'll want to interrogate him. Use exit five.

Yes, sir. On our way.

Braedon closed the connection and turned toward the old man. "Keep your voice to a whisper. What's your name?"

"Gunther."

"Gunther, take off your lab coat," Braedon commanded. He knelt and began removing Nick's military jacket, utility belt, and hat. Once finished, he handed them to the man and took the lab coat. "Put these on." Braedon wrapped Nick in the lab coat, making sure to cover his head.

He paused, his mind sifting through his options. *We need a ride. Someone close by.* He thought for a moment. *Jace! He's out doing deliveries. If he's close enough…* Braedon activated his implant. He let out a sigh of relief when Jace responded.

What's up, Braedon?

Jace! I've got an emergency! Are you anywhere near the Research and Records compound?

Yeah. I'm about a mile or two away. What's wrong?

No time for explanations. I need a pickup, now! Meet me at exit five on the West side of the building. Be ready for possible pursuit.

Pursuit? Yeah, okay. Oh, man, Braedon. What have you gotten yourself into?

See you in a few! Gotta go!

Braedon turned back to Gunther. He did a quick assessment of his appearance. "Your pants aren't the same color, but they're dark enough to not be too obvious."

"It's too small," Gunther whispered, pulling at the jacket to make it meet in the middle.

"It'll have to do," Braedon said as he unzipped his own jacket to match Gunther's. "Just follow my lead. The cameras are acting up. Is that your handiwork?"

"Probably a friend of mine did that."

"Nice. But they might still be able to hear us, so try not to talk." He grabbed a nearby cart and transferred the items from it onto one of the tables. "Nick, give me a hand," he said, his voice returning to normal volume. "Help me get this guy on the cart." He rolled it to where Nick's body lay. Together, Braedon and Gunther heaved him onto it. Braedon grabbed the satchel containing the weapon and placed it on the cart's bottom shelf. After that, he grabbed the white lab coat Gunther had been wearing and draped it over Nick's head and torso.

Braedon stepped closer to Gunther and whispered. "I don't know if all the cameras are scrambled, or when the techs might get them working again. So, when we leave this room, keep your head down so they can't get a good look at your face. If we meet anyone, just pretend you have a headache and keep looking down.

Don't say a word. The microphones will detect your voice. I'll lead. You push the cart."

Gunther nodded, his expression grim. After a moment's hesitation, he grabbed the cart and followed Braedon toward the exit.

Braedon focused on keeping his heart rate calm as he guided them through a maze of corridors, passed several doors, and into the elevator. His companion followed behind, pushing the cart, his knuckles white on the handle. *So far so good. God, keep the path clear before us.* They stepped off the elevator and into a maintenance hallway several floors down. Braedon's hands went cold as he spotted Captain Hubing waiting for them.

"It's about time you two arrived," the captain said, his face firm and businesslike as he glanced at the unmoving body on the cart.

"Sorry, captain. We got here as fast as we could," Braedon replied, not slowing his forward stride. As he had hoped, the captain turned his back to Gunther and fell into step beside Braedon.

"Commissioner Holst is furious. He's ordered us to investigate the security breach, but he also needs us to keep it quiet," the captain said, his irritation obvious. "Once the two of you finish cleaning up this mess, report to me for debriefing."

"Yes, sir. Did they find the mole?"

"Not yet. Whoever was sending the signal was good at covering himself. Until security finds him, the building is locked down tight. I have to personally talk to Riggs and Walker in order for you to leave. But don't say anything about this. I don't want them to know more than necessary."

Braedon felt the pressure in his chest ease. The captain kept walking, his eyes forward. *He didn't notice! No doubt the dim lighting helped. We might actually make it!*

They traveled down two more halls before the captain stopped them at a set of doors. "Wait here," he said. Braedon's heart skipped a beat as Hubing finally glanced at Gunther. Fortunately, the man was still following Braedon's instructions and had his head lowered.

"Szulcewski, what's wrong with you?"

Gunther glanced up slightly. It wasn't much, but just enough for the captain to realize something was amiss. Surprise registered on his face and he reached for his weapon.

Braedon grabbed his superior's arm, spun him around, and used the momentum to slam him against the wall. The captain went limp. Braedon caught his unconscious body and eased it to the floor, then resumed his place at the front of the cart. "C'mon, we're almost out."

"But ... but what are you g ... going to do? Just leave him lying here?" Gunther asked, his voice trembling. "And what about the guards? Now that we don't have him to move them out of our way, how will we get passed?"

"Leave that to me," Braedon replied. "Just keep going!"

Time was now against them. With any luck, the cameras were still on the fritz. But even if they didn't witness the attack on Captain Hubing, it probably wouldn't take long for someone to notice his body lying in the hallway.

Braedon and Gunther rounded the last corner and stepped into another hallway. The two men watching the door pointed their rifles in their direction. However, the moment they recognized Braedon, they lowered them and relaxed.

"Hey, Braedon, what's going on?" the first man asked, his face alert but confused at the sight of the body on the cart.

Braedon took a deep breath to quell his excitement. *Security hasn't warned them yet!* "There was a break-in," he replied. "This guy tried to steal some data from one of the labs. Unfortunately for him, the security techs tracked him down and sent us to deal with him."

The men exchanged glances as Braedon drew closer. He kept his eyes focused on their eyes, waiting for the inevitable realization of Gunther's identity.

"Poor schmuck," Riggs snickered. "Who'd be crazy enough to try to break into here?"

"Yeah, I know. Right?" Braedon agreed with a winning smile. "Well, the captain ordered us to take him to headquarters for questioning. So if you'll excuse us—"

"Wait a sec," Walker held up a hand. "We have to follow protocol. No one leaves without authorization from the captain. I'm surprised he's not here yet. He told us he was on his way. Let me check with him."

Braedon waited for Walker's eyes to lose their focus as he accessed his implant before he launched his attack. He landed a knockout blow against Walker's temple, then spun to face the other guard. Caught by surprise, Riggs barely reacted in time to ward off the first of Braedon's blows. He backpedaled frantically and raised his rifle toward his attacker. Braedon countered with a swift high kick, knocking the weapon out of his opponent's hands. Riggs growled in rage and lunged forward. Braedon ducked and cut the legs out from underneath his adversary with a sweep of his leg. Before Riggs could recover, Braedon knocked him unconscious with a punch.

"We're out of time!" Braedon said, jumping back to his feet. "Forget the cart. Let's move!" He grabbed the satchel from the bottom shelf and sprinted toward the doors. He placed his thumb onto the reader, then bolted through the exit the second it opened, not even looking to see if his companion was following.

Braedon searched the area for signs of attackers. The bluish moonlight from the Globe far above created eerie shadows everywhere. Suddenly, the headlights of an approaching vehicle illuminated the loading dock on which he and Gunther stood. The older man let out a small cry of fear as the vehicle came to a stop in front of them. Braedon turned toward him and placed a reassuring hand on his shoulder. "He's a friend! C'mon! Get in!"

The back door of the hovering vehicle popped open. Braedon cast a quick glance over his shoulder, then pushed Gunther forward. The two men dove into the back of the hovercar. Braedon slammed the door and called out, "Jace, go!"

Jace spun the vehicle around one hundred and eighty degrees and hit the accelerator. However, before the hovercar could clear the edge of the building, Braedon caught sight of movement on the wall. Fear nearly stopped his heart. The shadowy form of a man was clinging to it like a spider. Braedon pointed and called out a warning. "Left wall! Look out!"

The figure detached itself and fell to the street. It stood and blocked their path, seemingly unafraid of the approaching vehicle.

"What...what is that?" Gunther asked, his voice quaking.

"A Guardian!"

10

THE GUARDIAN

"Ram him!" Braedon called out. Jace hit the accelerator. The vehicle sped toward the black-clad soldier. Then, in an impossible display of acrobatics, the technologically-altered human flipped and landed on the hood of the speeding vehicle. Based on the velocity of their car, Braedon expected the man to slide off. However, as soon as the Guardian landed on his knees, he spread his arms out wide and stuck in place as if glued down.

"How…how is that possible?" Gunther asked.

"Specialized suits," Braedon said, more to himself than to Gunther's question. He tried to remember everything he'd learned about the suits and their possible weaknesses. With a wirelessly transmitted mental command, the Guardian could change the texture of the suit from a hard rubber-like substance that served as armor to the soft, flexible micro suction cups that allowed them to climb walls and stick to surfaces.

Braedon watched helplessly as the Guardian rolled his arms in an upward motion, releasing the suction of the suit from the hood and repositioning his arms into an upright stance. Once stable, the helmeted head snapped up to look at the occupants of the vehicle. Although the black V-shaped visor covered the man's entire face, Braedon could almost feel his gaze boring into him. The tight-fitting, solid black suit clung to the man's body, accentuating his bulging muscles and lean physique. *If it comes to a hand-to-hand fight, there's no way I'm winning*, Braedon realized with sudden clarity. *I've got to find another way to defeat him.*

The Guardian lifted his right arm and pointed his wrist-mounted laser toward the windshield. Jace let out a cry of alarm and swerved back and forth. The movement forced their attacker to drop back to the hood and focus his energy on retaining his balance.

"Keep it up," Braedon commanded as the car finally cleared the end of the alleyway. Jace pulled a hard right and turned onto one of the main city streets. Fortunately, since it was nearly midnight, traffic was sparse.

While Jace continued to swerve, Braedon climbed halfway out the window. He grabbed the car's frame with his left hand and fired the laser pistol in his right. The first few shots went wide of their target as the motion of the hovercar threw off his aim. The Guardian's helmet turned in Braedon's direction, but the erratic movements of the car kept him from returning fire. Braedon adjusted his aim, this time scoring several hits. With the Guardian's suit still in its softer form, the laser blasts tore large holes into his left shoulder. The Guardian lifted his right hand off the hood to fire back at Braedon. However, Jace's erratic driving kept the attacker's computer-enhanced brain from hitting his target.

"Hang on!" Jace suddenly shouted, causing Braedon and Gunther to both grab onto the seats in front of them. He slammed on the breaks and turned the wheel sharply. The change in speed and direction bent the man's body backward. The bones of any normal human would have snapped under the strain. For the Guardian, it only rendered him momentarily helpless.

"I can't keep this up forever! We've got to figure out how to get him off the hood!" Jace yelled, then hit the accelerator, sending the vehicle lurching forward.

Gunther suddenly dove into the front seat and grabbed a bottle of water resting in the cup holder.

"What are you doing?" Jace asked angrily as Gunther righted himself and unscrewed the lid. Gunther ignored the question, reached out the window and poured the liquid onto the hood just before the Guardian set his gloved hand down to renew his grip.

Jace's eyes lit up with sudden understanding. He swerved hard once more. The Guardian's weight shifted onto the water-soaked hood. He struggled to maintain his hold, but the next swerve from Jace sent him flying off the hood.

Braedon glanced at Gunther. "Good thinking." When he turned his attention back to their pursuer, he felt his stomach drop. "He's getting up! Jace, get us out of here!"

The Guardian jumped to his feet and ran toward the speeding vehicle, seemingly uninjured despite the awkward fall.

"I'm trying," Jace shot back. "But there's a batch of late-night traffic ahead! Unless you want me to crash headlong into the oncoming row of traffic, we're just going to have to wait a second for an opening!"

"Push the cars in front of us if you have to! The Guardian's coming up fast!" Braedon shouted. He leaned out the window and fired several more shots at their attacker. He expected the man to try to evade the shots. Instead, he simply raised his arm and blocked them.

"The suit has changed into its armored form," Gunther advised. "With the metal lacing the skin on his arm and his enhanced reflexes, your shots won't do any damage!"

"I'm aware of that!" Braedon said through gritted teeth as he kept firing. "But it might keep him off balance"

Jace finally pushed past the cars in front of them and hit the accelerator.

Braedon let out a growl of frustration. "He's just too fast! With his speed *and* agility, he's keeping up with us!" He continued his barrage of blaster fire, but Jace's driving and the risk of hitting civilians disrupted his accuracy.

"Where are we going?" Gunther asked.

"It doesn't matter if we can't lose this guy. We've got to shake him before the police arrive. Then find a place—"

"Look out!"

A large truck came out of a cross street directly into their path. Jace yanked the wheel hard to the right, avoiding a full sideways collision. However, the sudden turn sent them careening wildly out of control. The corner of the hovercar hit the edge of a parked van, spinning it sideways and bringing it to a full stop.

"Everyone all right?" Braedon asked, his own senses rattled. Both Jace and Gunther replied in the affirmative. A laser blast flew past the hood of the car, barely missing it and colliding with a nearby building. Braedon turned to look in the direction from which the shot originated. The Guardian was quickly closing the distance between them.

"Jace, get us out of here!" Braedon yelled as he sent several more shots at their pursuer.

Jace slammed on the accelerator, catapulting them down the street. However, before they had gone more than one hundred feet, a laser blast struck the back window. Braedon ducked as shards of reinforced duraglass flew in all directions. Jace cried out in pain as several pieces cut his neck and face.

"Ahhh!" Gunther shouted in alarm as the hovercar slid sideways into the edge of a building. The car shuddered as it came to a stop once more. Another laser blast hit the back of the vehicle, causing the gravity control units to fail. The vehicle dropped heavily to the ground with a deep thud.

The car is shot! We have to make a run for it. He glanced at Jace. The man was groaning and beginning to stir. *He won't be able to make it. But he might get away if Gunther and I distract the Guardian.*

Braedon grabbed the satchel containing the stolen weapon, bolted out of the car, and flung open the passenger door. He grabbed Gunther's shoulder and pulled him into an upright position. "Can you run?"

Gunther stared blankly for a moment, then blinked and nodded. "Yes, I…I think so."

"Follow me!" he commanded. He grabbed Gunther by the arm and ran toward a nearby alley. He fought to keep from tripping over the debris hidden in the deep shadows created by the bluish light from the Globe.

"What…about…Jace?" Gunther asked as they ran, his breathing already heavy from the unexpected exercise.

"He's unconscious. He should be okay once we're gone. The Guardian doesn't care about him. He's after us."

Braedon glanced behind him as he ran. The Guardian suddenly appeared at the entrance to the alley just fifty feet away. "Keep running!" Braedon urged. He stopped running and sent several shots at their pursuer.

The Guardian sprinted toward him, blocking the laser blasts with uncanny precision. Braedon threw down his weapon and the satchel and moved into a martial-arts ready position. Beside him, Gunther took cover behind a dumpster.

Although the Guardian was slightly taller, Braedon still used his impressive six-foot-one-inch frame to its fullest advantage. Unable to match the man's strength, Braedon moved in close to his attacker and attempted to throw him off balance. Braedon ducked under the man's punch, then used his right arm to push against the Guardian's chest while simultaneously kicking his leg out from under him. The armored soldier crashed to the ground and Braedon struck out at the man's neck.

However, his blows seemed to have no effect. The Guardian was back on his feet faster than Braedon thought possible. Braedon dodged several punches and spun away from his attacker. He caught sight of Gunther coming out from his hiding place and reaching for the satchel.

Braedon circled around so the other would have his back toward the scientist. He dove in once more to attack. This time, however, the Guardian anticipated the move. He landed a swift blow to the side of Braedon's head. Braedon stumbled and fell to the ground. He leaned against the wall and fought to clear his head. The Guardian spun to face Gunther, who now held the stolen weapon in his hands. The armored warrior sent the gun flying with a swift kick, leaving Gunther defenseless.

Braedon tried to focus, but the blow had shaken him. He could only watch the inevitable outcome. He had failed.

A blast of electricity suddenly lit up the darkness and struck the Guardian. The enhanced soldier stood immobile for a moment before collapsing to the ground.

A man materialized from the shadows. In his hands was a large weapon pointed directly at Gunther.

11

THE SAFE HOUSE

"We've gotta move quickly," the man said as he ran over to where Braedon lay on the ground. "The Volt's effects won't keep the Guardian down for long."

"Steven!" Braedon breathed in relief. "How did you...?" The question died on his lips as he noticed the strange distortion of light around his mentor's shoulders. As Steven moved, the cloak's *appearance* changed, causing him to nearly disappear into his surroundings. The disorienting sensation was enhanced by the Globe's ghostly light.

Steven set his weapon on the ground and helped Braedon stand. His gaze swept the alley.

"We need to move," he said, his voice deep and resonant. "The Guardian's computer systems will reboot in a minute or two, and the Volt takes longer than that to charge. Can you walk?"

"Yeah, but give me a moment. That last punch really rattled me."

Steven grabbed two bundles from near the wall. "Put this on. We've gotta get out of here before—" The distant sound of sirens filled the air, adding urgency to his words.

Braedon grabbed one of the bundles—another cloak identical to the one Steven wore—and threw it around his shoulders.

Steven reached into a pocket and withdrew several small round devices. He gave a handful to Braedon, then turned to Gunther. He placed another cloak around the man's shoulders and attached two of the devices to the stunned scientist's chest, waist, knees, and finally his forehead. Familiar with the tech, Braedon followed suit.

"What are these for?" Gunther asked as he studied the strange material of the cloak.

"They're mini cameras," Steven replied. "The images they capture are projected onto the back of the cloak. If you stand still or move very slowly, you will effectively become invisible. It's extremely useful under poor lighting conditions."

"But they don't cover the front!"

"Right. Which is why we keep our backs to the street. Since you won't be able to see me, follow my verbal cues."

"What about Jace? We can't just leave him!" Braedon stated.

"Cameron went to help him," Steven said. "We were following you. When you ran from the crash site, I followed. Cameron stayed to help Jace. We'll meet up with them later." He grabbed the hood of the cloak and pulled it over his head, indicating for the others to do the same. Once they were ready, Steven led the way.

He brought them to a halt at the end of the alley with a whispered command. "Stop here. Keep your body facing the wall, including your head. All of the cameras must face the same direction for the camouflage effect to work. When you reach the corner, turn your body quickly so you stay parallel with the wall. Move at a steady walking speed. Not too fast."

Steven led the way and was the first to round the corner. After a moment, he called quietly for Gunther to follow. Although it was only a few seconds before Steven urged Braedon to proceed, the ever-increasing volume of the approaching sirens made time seem to stretch. When it was his turn to move, he felt as if every pair of eyes within a mile was focused in his direction. Having his back to the street turned out to be not only disconcerting but very disorienting. He fought with every ounce of his will to keep from turning his head to look behind him.

"We're almost there," Steven said from somewhere to Braedon's left. "Just keep following the wall a few more feet then turn another corner."

The three cloaked men proceeded around the new corner in the same fashion as before. Finally, after several more torturous seconds, Steven gave them permission to remove their cloaks.

They were in another darkened alley a block from the original scene of the confrontation. A crowd had now gathered in the streets, causing the newly arrived police officers to spend several minutes corralling the spectators. With their attention thus diverted, the officers never saw the three cloaked me stroll out of the alley and walk away from the area.

Once they reached a residential section of the city, Gunther broke the silence. "Where are we going now?"

"There's a safe house nearby," Steven replied as he led them past several homes. "We'll spend the night there."

Steven led them to the back door of a small house with a well-manicured lawn and wooden fence. Glancing around one last time, he placed his thumb on the reader and opened the door. Once they were inside, they removed their cloaks and the miniature cameras. They set them on a nearby table, then Steven led Braedon and Gunther down a set of stairs into a well-furnished basement. He lit a single lamp and urged the other men to sit on one of the pieces of plush furniture.

Braedon and Gunther sank heavily onto the couch and armchair, the soft cushions kneading the tension from the evening's activities out of their bodies. While they relaxed, Steven reached into the freezer section of a nearby refrigerator and withdrew an ice pack. He handed it to Braedon, who gratefully accepted it. He placed it against the side of his head to ease the swelling from the Guardian's blow. Steven reached into the refrigerator once more and withdrew three bottles of cold water. He tossed one to each of them, opened the third, took a huge drink, and sat down on a wooden chair facing Gunther.

"Now that we're no longer trying to evade capture, let me formally introduce myself," Steven began. "I'm Steven Russell, 3rd Gen. Nice to meet you."

The older man smiled slightly, the evening's activities had clearly taken their toll on him. "Gunther Lueschen, 1st Gen, 197. Thank you for saving us back there." He turned his attention to Braedon. "And thank you for saving me in the lab, not to mention getting me out of there. I owe you my life."

Braedon leaned forward in his chair. "You're most welcome. I'm Braedon Lewis, 1st Gen, 192."

Steven let out a deep sigh. "I'm sure you both are exhausted and would like to get some sleep, but I think you'll agree we've got some important issues to discuss. And one amazing story to tell. Mr. Lueschen, if I were in your shoes, I'd be wondering exactly who we are and why we helped you. We'll share that, but only if we're convinced we can trust you. Since we're the ones who rescued you, I hope you'll agree it makes sense for you to go first."

Gunther nodded. "Yes, I agree." He took a long drink of water and inhaled deeply. "I'm a particle physicist. I had been working on the Portal Research project since…well, it had been a few years. But Travis discovered—"

"—who's Travis?" Braedon asked.

"He's my colleague." Gunther stared at the floor for a moment before continuing. "I'm sorry. Tonight's activities have shaken me. And there's so much to tell. Perhaps I should just start at the beginning. I arrived in Tartarus five years ago…"

Despite his weariness, Gunther forced himself to relate his tale. Yet even as he spoke, the memories brought a fresh wave of pain. "My nephew, Erik, and I decided to take another one of our hiking trips into the forest. We disregarded the warnings about the disappearances and the mysterious portals. After all, we'd been doing this for years. It had become an annual tradition ever since his father had died. I'll regret that decision for the rest of my life. The portal snagged both of us."

Gunther's voice trailed off as he relived the horrifying experience. He shivered from the memory. Next came the traumatic realization they were trapped in an underground world and he would possibly never see his wife again. But at least he had Erik to comfort him in those early days. That was until…

12

TRAGIC TIDINGS

Gunther opened the front door of the apartment he and Erik had been given since arriving in Elysium three years prior. "Erik, are you here?" he called out as he absentmindedly dropped his brief-case and jacket onto the couch. When no reply came, Gunther frowned. *His shoes and uniform are still here. It's not like him to leave without them.* "Erik?" he tried once more as he headed toward the kitchen. Erik was sitting at the table, his elbows resting on the polished black surface and his hands covering his face.

"What's wrong?" Gunther asked in concern.

Erik looked up at his uncle in surprise. Based on his expression, it was clear he had been so lost in thought he never heard the other enter the apartment. "What? Oh, hey, Uncle Gun. I didn't realize you were home. I…I've just got a lot on my mind right now."

"Yeah, I've noticed you've been pretty distracted lately," Gunther said as grabbed one of the chairs and sat next to his nephew. "Does this have something to do with your recent assignment? I mean, I know joining the Elysium Security Force was an import-ant step in helping you recover from transition depression, but I don't want you to feel you have to do it out of some sense of ob-ligation. There are other ways you can contribute to this society."

Erik leaned back in his chair, his gaze unfocused. "No, it's not that."

Gunther paused, uncertain how far to press the issue. "Don't forget what Haley said at our last group session. 'It's better to talk openly about things than to bottle your feelings up inside.'"

Erik rolled his eyes. "Yeah, I know. They've been feeding us those same lines since the day we woke up in this nightmare." Although Gunther knew the words of the counselor were true in principle, he had to agree with his nephew that at times, they seemed like hollow platitudes.

Erik continued, "Sorry, Uncle Gun. It's just…I miss home. I miss Megan, even after all this time. We would've been married by now, and…maybe even had our first kid. I just can't move on," he said, his eyes tearing up. "Sometimes, the pain and loss are just so unbearable. The only thing that even keeps me going is the fact I'm involved in the ESF…and you, of course."

Erik stood and walked to the window. He stared out at the city, the light from the Globe reflecting off of the purplish walls of the cavern far in the distance. "I understand why so many people lose themselves in computer-generated, virtual worlds or give in to alcoholism. Some days I think I'd rather be anywhere or do anything than be stuck here." He looked at his uncle. His expression was filled with such pain and aching loneliness Gunther had to struggle to keep his own grief from surfacing.

"Erik, I completely understand," Gunther said. He stood and stepped closer to his nephew. "But we can't lose hope. Listen, I know it's hard sometimes. Even though I've only been working on the government's Portal Research Project for a couple of months, we've made some major advancements. Up to this point, they didn't have anyone who was trained in particle physics. Since I've come on board, I've been able to show them things that have progressed their research tremendously. I'm very optimistic we can find a way to reverse the portals!"

"But what good would that do?" Erik replied, his face still reflecting his doubt. "Even if you could stabilize the portals and get us back to Earth, we're still almost two hundred years in the future! Everything we knew—our homes, our families, our loved ones—they're all dead and gone!" As he spoke, the tone of his voice became edgier, his frustration and hopelessness coloring his words.

Gunther looked imploringly at this young man who had become like a son to him. "Yes, we have traveled into the future, but that's exactly the point. The portals that brought us here traversed both space and time. If we can just figure out how, we should be able to alter the space-time continuum to take us backward. And how do we even know *we're* the ones who have traveled into the future? All the citizens of Tartarus know is that two hundred years have passed since the first people arrived. But how do we know the portals didn't send them backward in time? Time appears to work differently here. We came through in 2047, only thirty-nine years after George Mathison disappeared from Earth. But almost two hundred years have passed here since he arrived."

Erik shook his head, unconvinced. He brushed past Gunther and sat back down on the chair near the table. "'*If* we can …,' 'we *should* be able …,' all you have is wishful thinking. Don't get me wrong. I know if anyone can do it, you can. But even with your knowledge, it's still a long shot. We have to face the harsh reality we're never going back! Maybe we should take Haley's advice and *embrace* our life in Elysium instead of obsessing over finding a way home."

Gunther pointed a finger at Erik, his anger rising. "I don't ever want to hear you say that again! I will *never* give up on finding a way to get back to your Aunt Eveleen!"

Erik flinched. "I'm sorry. It's just...while *you* have something to strive for, the rest of us just waste away our time."

"Then maybe that's the answer," Gunther said. "You need 'something to strive for.' You need to make a difference. As good as the ESF has been for you, being a police officer just isn't the same as being a marine on Earth. Maybe you should...I don't know, look for something else to fulfill you, something where you feel like you're making a difference."

Erik was silent as he considered his uncle's words. "Maybe you're right," he said at last. "I do need a change. I need to feel like I'm accomplishing something important. I can't just sit around doing nothing more than giving speeding tickets and helping Box junkies find their way home." Erik glanced at the clock mounted on the wall. He shot a weak grin at his uncle as he stood. "Thanks for the encouragement. I'm gonna take a quick shower before I have to report for duty."

As Erik headed toward the bathroom, Gunther called out one last bit of advice. "Hang in there, son. I'll find a way to get us back to earth, even if I have to die trying. I promise. Things are going to get better."

The doorbell rang, startling Gunther and waking him from his evening nap. He glanced at the clock and frowned. *Who could that be at this hour? Probably just another drunk,* he thought irritably. He climbed out of his favorite chair and walked toward the door. However, his demeanor sobered at the sight of a woman and two men who appeared on the monitor built into the inside of the door. The woman was Haley, his government-appointed counselor, but the other two wore uniforms.

Gunther's heartbeat quickened. These weren't typical ESF uniforms either; they were the black, purple, and silver uniforms of the Elysium Elite Corps. After the conversation he and Erik had three months ago, Erik had taken his uncle's advice and submitted his application to join the Elite Corps, the branch of the ESF focused on protecting Elysium's interests abroad. The recruiters seemed thrilled at Erik's qualifications and accepted his application almost immediately. Since then, he had been gone frequently, traveling to one or more of the other main territories. Sometimes, his unit even ventured into the numerous settlements spread out in caverns and tunnels between the main inhabited areas of Tartarus.

Gunther took a deep breath and fought to control the sudden shaking in his hands. He pressed the corner of the touch-sensitive panel on the wall that opened the door.

"Good evening, Gunther," Haley said politely. "We're sorry to bother you so late, but we need to talk to you about an important matter. May we come inside?"

Gunther nodded his assent and stepped aside to allow the three of them to enter. Once they were inside, he closed the door and led the small group into the adjoining living room. He gestured for them to sit on the couch, then sank numbly into his chair, dread weighing heavily upon him. Haley sat on the far side of the couch to Gunther's left, and the two men sat on the far right.

Haley leaned forward as she spoke, her face full of compassion, "Gunther, as you probably already know, these men are from the Elysium Elite Corps. They have something to share with you about Erik."

Gunther felt his gut twist in pain. *Oh no, not Erik! Please, not Erik!*

The older of the two men took off his hat. He cleared his throat and addressed Gunther. "Mr. Lueschen, there was an attack on Erik's unit stationed outside the city of Bab al-Jihad. A contingent of jihadist terrorists ambushed them and killed seven of our men…including your nephew."

Gunther felt his whole body begin to shake uncontrollably as the terrible truth sank in. His mind reeled and he became oblivious to his surroundings. Even Haley's gentle touch on his knee went completely unnoticed.

Erik was gone.

Overwhelmed by sorrow, Gunther wept. Haley crouched next to his chair and placed her arm around his shoulder. Though she spoke words of comfort, they fell on deaf ears.

He was now alone, truly alone, with only his hopes to sustain him.

13

GROWING UNEASE

Gunther paused his account of past events. The pain of Erik's loss washed over him once again. Braedon and Steven remained silent, as if giving him time to work through his grief. Although he had only summarized the events for them, his heart reopened the memories in full detail. *How can it still hurt so much after all these years?*

Gunther took another drink before continuing his narrative. "After Erik's death, I spent the next two years pouring myself into my work. I had nothing else to live for. My best friend, Travis Butler, helped me through. But a few months ago, they pulled me from the Portal Research and assigned me to the Guardian program as Travis's assistant. At first I was enamored with the possibilities. It blinded me to the…moral implications of what we were trying to accomplish. After several months, my unease grew."

Another memory surfaced. The conversation he'd had with Travis in the Heavenly Helpings restaurant just a week ago echoed in his mind like it was yesterday.

"So you're looking more glum than usual," Travis said. "Is something new bothering you or just, you know, the normal stuff?"

Gunther frowned as he absentmindedly stirred his coffee with a spoon. "Well, there's always the normal stuff. But yes, there is something new." Setting the spoon down, he looked up at his friend as he searched for the right words to explain his feelings. "I don't know. You're native born, so you don't understand the desire us 1st Generationists have to return to Earth. This isn't our home."

Travis nodded. "Yeah, I can imagine it's hard for you, especially since your wife is there. But as I've told you before, you have to trust the wisdom of the Celestials. They brought you here for a reason, just like everyone else."

Gunther's frown deepened. "You know I don't buy into that 'Celestials' bologna. Why would aliens go through all of the trouble to transport specific humans from Earth in order to save our species? Why would they care? And if they did, then what if they're not benevolent? What if they're keeping us as lab experiments or for food or who knows what? If they are real, then why don't they communicate with us? There's not one shred of evidence that they even exist."

"Well, suit yourself, but I at least find the idea comforting," Travis replied. "It gives my life meaning when I think that the survival of mankind may depend in part on me."

"Anyway," Gunther replied, steering the conversation back to the main point to avoid any further 'religious' discussions, "I've been really struggling these past couple months since they took me off of the Portal Research Project." Leaning over the table, he lowered his voice so that only his friend could hear. "It almost feels like the government pulled the rug out from under us just when we were on the verge of a major breakthrough. Have you ever experienced anything like that in your Guardian research?"

Travis shot his friend a disbelieving look. He took a sip of his coffee before answering, "C'mon, Gunther. I've known you for almost three and a half years. In all that time, I've never seen you as one of those conspiracy theorist types. Sure there have been cuts and changes in the Guardian program over the years, but the rationale we receive from the higher-ups always makes sense. They've got the bigger picture in mind. You know as well as I do that as scientists, we often get so wrapped up in our research we become too narrowly focused."

"If it were only that, I might agree with you," Gunther said. "But there's something else that bothers me. Now that I'm working on research for the Type I Guardian, I've found myself growing more and more concerned."

"Concerned? About what?"

"Tell me honestly, Travis. Have you ever wondered if what we're doing is right?" Gunther asked, his expression troubled. "I mean, I'm all for human technological enhancements and such, but what about some of the other stuff? I was reading an article the other day about the Trait Selection program for expecting parents. Don't you think there's something wrong with treating children like they are consumer products we can improve, modify, and evaluate according to some idealistic standard?"

"Gunther, you sound like one of those religious prudes." Travis laughed. "I can tell ya, when Sandy and I had our children, it was fantastic being able to weed out any bad genes and also be able to choose the sex, hair color, eye color, you name it! We were able to get the children we'd always dreamed of. What's wrong with that? You 1st Geners really need to learn to let go of some of your old-fashioned ideas."

Gunther's face reflected his skepticism. "Maybe so, but don't you think some of the new choices are disturbing?"

Travis shrugged. "Why settle for just the basics when we can improve the human species? Why settle for natural selection when we can use artificial selection to speed up the evolutionary process? Besides, what's 'wrong' for you may not be 'wrong' for someone else."

"But that's just the point!" Gunther shot back. "What one person thinks of as an improvement might be different from someone else's definition of the word. We may think it's an improvement now, but what's going to happen in fifty or one hundred years? We're the guinea pigs in our own experiments. And if we decide in a few decades we don't like the results of the experiment, it may be too late to reverse the process. We scientists are often so busy trying to find out if we can do something we fail to ask whether we should do it. Don't you think mixing human and animal DNA messes with the very definition of human?"

Travis leaned back as a server arrived with their food, leaving Gunther's question unanswered for the time being. After they had had a few minutes to enjoy their meal, Travis picked up their conversation, his expression more serious. "Listen, Gunther, the stuff we've been able to achieve in the Guardian program has been amazing. We've actually succeeded in giving some of these soldiers the ability to see in the dark, an enhanced sense of smell and hearing, and superhuman strength. And that's just the beginning. However, I'm not going to lie to you. Any time you're working with altering the genes of a human, you're going to make some mistakes. Most of them show up pretty quickly in the specimen's life, but sometimes the problems don't show up until it has developed for a few years."

Gunther raised a finger. "Aha. See, you just called this human an 'it.' That's another step in dehumanizing people."

Travis finished the last of his griblin chops and smirked. "Okay, okay. So I made a little slip. But don't you think the ends justify the means?"

"Frankly, I don't," Gunther replied. "Maybe I am just too old fashioned, but I don't think we should be playing God with human lives. Where does it end? Already some enhanced children that have the new wireless implants are becoming more prideful and disrespectful toward their elders because they feel superior. And in many ways, they are! They can access data straight from the central network to their brains and do amazing computations that leave us 'naturals' in the dust. What kind of effect is that going to have on society? Doesn't it cause you concern that we're already starting to see the formation of two new classes of people—the enhanced and the naturals? Add those that are genetically altered into the mix, and we have a truly frightening social experiment on our hands. If you believe we can 'save' mankind through tinkering with nature, you haven't taken a hard enough look at the kind of barbarism mankind is capable of."

Travis dismissed his friend's concerns with a wave of his hand. "You're so pessimistic. That's why we have leaders such as Governor Mathison. He keeps a tight rein on the technology and won't let *things get out of hand. Which, again, is why we shouldn't worry too much when we don't understand why the government puts an end to certain projects. They're responsible for paving the way for the future and making sure that every step is well thought out and safe."*

Gunther snorted in derision. "You have way too much faith in humans. There's an old saying on earth that says, 'Power corrupts, and absolute power corrupts absolutely.' It seems ingrained in our human nature to become corrupted by power, especially politicians. Don't get me wrong. Mathison seems like a pretty straightforward guy, but that's part of the problem. He seems too good. He's an idealist who's trying to make a utopia. People like that can become the worst kinds of dictators—those that will do all sorts of atrocities because they justify them as being for the 'good of society.'"

Travis emptied his coffee cup, then shook his head and laughed lightly. "Have you been listening to one of those 'preachers' from that Crimson Liberty terrorist group? You make it sound like he's suddenly going to become like...like...that guy from Earth who killed all of those Jewish people. What was his name?"

"Adolf Hitler." Gunther offered.

"Yeah, Hitler."

"Well, can you at least do me one favor?" Gunther asked hesitantly. "Would you...is there a way you could ask around—discreetly, of course—to find out about the Portal Research Project? I really want to know if they're even still working on finding a way to get us back to Earth."

"Sure thing. I'll see what I can dig up and get back to you."

"Travis was true to his word," Gunther said, the memory fading. "But nothing I had imagined prepared me for what he would find."

Braedon and Steven leaned forward, both completely engrossed in the story. Gunther's expression darkened. "He discovered the government wasn't really interested in opening the portals back to Earth. That wasn't their goal. It was just a cover story to keep us working."

Gunther nodded toward the satchel resting on the floor. "They were using our research to create that: a deadly weapon. A weapon to help them win the war they are about to launch!"

14

CRIMSON LIBERTY

Braedon exchanged glances with Steven. "So we were right. Mathison's really going to do it."

Steven turned to Gunther. "What does the weapon do?"

"I don't know. We weren't able to find out. All I know is it carries the codename, 'Vortex'." Gunther shifted his gaze to Braedon. "Do you still have the data stick from the lab?"

Braedon nodded.

"That should contain the information we need."

Steven furrowed his brows. "So you risked your life to break into the Research and Records compound to steal this weapon. But why? What do you plan to do with it?"

Braedon spoke before Gunther could answer. "You told me back in the lab you could use it to reverse the portals back to Earth. Can you do that?"

Gunther winced slightly. "I believe so. I wasn't really after the weapon. I was trying to recover the original prototype we created to stabilize the portals. However, when I got to the lab, it had disappeared. Since this weapon was based on those plans, I believe I can use the data I downloaded to alter the weapon and complete the design. *That's* why I broke into the compound."

Braedon blew out a sigh. "It's nice to know I didn't blow my cover for nothing. But tell me, how did you get past security? We figured someone had to be helping you."

"Yes," Gunther said. "Travis had a friend who worked in security. He helped Travis gain the original info, and also helped me make it as far as I did."

"Let's hope he made it out," Braedon said. "What about Travis? Where is he?"

"He left the city," Gunther explained. "He said he was headed for Dehali. He was afraid the government would catch him and hurt his wife and children."

Steven leaned back in his chair. "Well, Gunther, we're certainly glad you're safe. If anyone but Braedon had been on duty tonight, you'd have been caught."

"An amazing coincidence," Gunther said.

"Or providence. Mr. Lueschen, you may be the answer to years of prayers. If there is even a chance you can get the portals stabilized, then I can promise you the full backing of our entire organization."

"Organization?" Gunther asked, somewhat taken aback by Steven's serious demeanor.

"Yes. Braedon and I both belong to Crimson Liberty."

Gunther stiffened at the name. Steven smiled wryly. "I see our reputation precedes us," he said, his voice laced with frustration.

"But you're a religious terrorist organization," Gunther stammered in confusion.

"I see you've been listening to the media," Braedon commented. "All the news feeds are under the control of Mathison's government, and as you've witnessed first-hand, they aren't the most reliable source of information. They tell people what they want the people to hear. They don't like what we stand for, so they paint us as an extremist group and blame all sorts of atrocities on us. In the war of appearances, they certainly have the upper hand."

"If you're not a terrorist organization, then what do you stand for?" Gunther said, somewhat apprehensive.

"Too often people only hear what we're against instead of what we're for," Steven said. "We believe all men and women are created equal by God, all life is precious, and all mankind should be allowed to live out their faith in public without fear of government reprisal."

Gunther's frown deepened. "That sounds reasonable. Why would the government label you a terrorist organization?"

"Because as you've seen, the government has an agenda," Steven stated. "They're not just content with building roads and keeping the peace. Since taking office nearly ten years ago, Mathison has been pushing legislation after legislation through the Congress to slowly erode our freedoms. And of course, it was all in the name of preserving the 'jewel that is Elysium.' Your story is a perfect example. The government knew you and your team had found a way to possibly stabilize the portals. But rather than continue to develop the technology, they converted it into a weapon."

"Mr. Lueschen—" Braedon began.

"Please, call me Gunther," he interjected.

Braedon smiled, then continued. "You're 1st Gen, right? You said you arrived in 197, so you lived most of your life on Earth. Mathison is showing the same kind of mentality Hitler showed just prior to World War II."

Gunther harrumphed. "Interesting. Travis made a similar comparison."

Braedon continued. "If he's allowed to continue down this path, there'll soon be no way to stop him. There's a famous quote from a Lutheran pastor named Martin Niemoller who lived at that time.

He said, 'When they came for the Jews, I did nothing, for I am not a Jew. When they came for the Socialists, I did nothing, for I am not a Socialist. When they came for the labor leaders, the homosexuals, the gypsies, I did nothing, for I am none of these, and when they came for me, I was alone, there was no one to stand up for me.'"

Steven looked at Gunther intensely as he picked up where Braedon left off. "With that quote in mind, many of us in Crimson Liberty *have* been speaking out against Mathison's policies for years, often at a heavy price. Several of us tried to convince the public that in order for a society to be free, dissent must be tolerated in the public square. Our message was mostly rejected, and we were labeled as 'bigots' and 'intolerant' by the media and social elites. Even many in our own churches didn't listen to us. And, unfortunately, our words turned out to be frighteningly prophetic."

"How so?" Gunther asked.

Steven sighed heavily. "In the last few years, the government has been working covertly to silence any opposition, forcing us to go underground. We fear Mathison has gained so much power there's very little we can do to stop him from taking complete control of the entire city."

Gunther's complexion suddenly drained of color. Braedon and Steven noticed the change in his countenance and exchanged glances.

"What is it?" Braedon asked in concern. "You had that same look on your face when I first found you in the lab."

Gunther looked back and forth between the two men. "It's already too late."

"Why?" Steven said, his voice low. "What did you discover?"

"I didn't mention it when I told you my story because I wasn't sure if I could completely trust you. But after what you just told me," Gunther swallowed hard before continuing, "at the rate things are going, Mathison will be able to control the minds of the people of Elysium within less than a year."

"Control their minds?" Braedon asked in astonishment. "How?"

"He's going to do it by using the implants from Pandora's Box!"

15

RISING STAKES

Braedon and Steven stared at Gunther in surprise and shock. Braedon was the first to recover. "The Pandora's Box implants? Are you sure it's just those? What about the regular wireless ones? And how could they control people through the implants anyway?"

"As far as the 'how' goes, it appears Mathison's people helped develop the technology. They put within each implant a back door allowing a central computer to override any other signals. Because the implants are connected directly to the brain, commands from Mathison would be indistinguishable from the person's own thoughts. He'll basically be able to create an army of human robots! Based on what little I read, it doesn't appear the regular wireless implants would work. The Pandora's Box implants are much more complex and connect to more parts of the brain."

Steven leaned back, his face reflecting the weariness of one who had grown tired of fighting. "This is worse than we had guessed," he said, turning toward Braedon. "We should've known his ambition would extend beyond the creation of the Guardians. We never dreamed he would turn his own citizens into soldiers."

"So you knew he was planning to attack the jihadists?" Gunther asked in surprise.

"Yes," Braedon said. "I suppose we should fill you in on our side of the story." He quickly recounted the events of the past eight years since his arrival in Tartarus. When he had finished, Gunther smiled wistfully.

"I wish I had known about your organization sooner. It would have made things much easier. I almost had a heart attack when you and your partner burst into the room. Speaking of which, how did you find me? What gave me away?"

Braedon took another swig of water before answering. "The security techs noticed someone was transmitting from an encrypted frequency. It took them a little while, but they finally figured out where the signal was being received. They sent Nick and I to check it out. When we didn't find you the first time, we were told to leave and then double back once the techs were able to shut down the transmission. As you learned first-hand, it worked."

Gunther ran his hand through his thinning hair as he processed Braedon's words. "And so, I suppose when you heard me muttering about being able to stabilize the portals and saw I had downloaded the data, you figured this would be a 'once in a lifetime' chance. You could use my failed infiltration attempt as a cover-up to escape from the compound."

"Yep. And it worked like a charm," Braedon commented with a tired grin. Steven harrumphed loudly. Taking mock offense, Braedon turned toward his mentor. "Hey, I got us out, didn't I?"

"Yeah," Steven replied. "But you wouldn't have made it very far if Jace hadn't been close enough to come pick you up when you called him."

"Called him?" Gunther asked, the lines in his forehead increasing. "But I didn't ... oh. I see. You have a wireless implant. So that's how you communicated with your commander. But aren't those against your religion? I mean, no offense, but I assumed you turned down the chance to become a Guardian because of your religious convictions."

Braedon sighed before answering. "Having a wireless implant isn't specifically against any direct teaching of Christianity. However, I wish I could go back and undo it. I got it prior to my change of heart. Regardless, there's a huge difference between having a small device embedded into your skin and having scientists and technicians encase your arms and legs with metal and play God with your body. You of all people should know what they do to those men. Didn't you say you worked on the Guardian program?"

Gunther looked embarrassed. "Yes, unfortunately. From what I know, it's a good thing you didn't agree to join the project. Travis confided in me he sometimes wondered if the Cyborgs, as you call them, had any humanity left. The technological implants make them too much like machines. They rarely speak and are almost too efficient in everything they do. They lack compassion and become disassociated with their families and friends."

Braedon's thoughts drifted toward Kyler. He missed his friend and wondered what had become of him. Was there anything left of the man he once knew? A disturbing thought struck him. *Could Kyler have been the Guardian who attacked us?*

Steven leaned forward so his elbows rested on his knees. He looked first at Braedon before turning his gaze to Gunther. "The bottom line regarding most technology is it's neither good nor evil. It's a tool. Technology has a way of bringing out what lies within the human heart. A knife can either cut food or kill a man. A hammer can build a home or destroy a life. Take Pandora's Box for example. In the hands of one man, it could be a powerful educational tool used to teach history, or it could help someone overcome their fears by facing them in a virtual world. In the hands of another man, it could be used for perverse pleasures and self-glorifying fantasies, often leading to destroyed personal relationships and the collapse of social functions in the real world."

The image of the woman Braedon helped while in his Pandora's Box session came unbidden to his mind. With it came the memory of his attraction to her and the disturbing thoughts that accompanied it.

"I see what you mean," Gunther stated. The tone of his voice made it clear he had had a similar experience. "Sadly, it appears to me the average human heart is selfish and lacking in self-control. Otherwise there wouldn't be so many Box rehabilitation centers, and the government wouldn't need to regulate it."

"Ain't that the truth," Braedon chimed in. "'Public virtue cannot exist in a nation without private virtue, and public virtue is the only foundation of republics.'"

"What was that?" Gunther asked, looking over at Braedon curiously.

"It's just a quote from John Adams my father drilled into me time and time again," Braedon replied. "Adams was one of the founding fathers of the United States and its second president," he explained for Steven's sake.

"If only more people understood that," Steven commented dryly. "They don't realize if they fail to control themselves, the government has to step in and do it. When that happens, people lose their freedom. The current culture of Elysium is one where people don't think things through rationally. They just follow their impulses. Many have become so addicted to instant gratification, mindless entertainment, and physical stimulation they've lost the ability to function properly in the real world. Have you met any addicts, Gunther?"

"Not personally, no," he replied.

Steven's expression reflected the pain in his soul. "These poor people have lost their will to live outside of the Box. They walk around like mindless zombies. When they first arrive at the reha-bilitation centers, we have to actually feed them, or they wouldn't eat. Even those who aren't addicts have problems thinking clearly. I've talked to so many people that just live in the moment. And it's not only the young people. Many adults have forgotten how to think rationally. Instead of seeing 'through' the eye and *with* the conscience, they see 'with' the eye *devoid* of a conscience. They think with their emotions. If something *feels* comfortable, no mat-ter how illogical it may be, they believe it to be true."

"So is there any hope for Elysium?" Gunther asked sincerely. "How do you propose to change the culture? By imposing your beliefs upon them?"

Braedon seemed somewhat irritated by the scientist's tone. But before he could say anything, Steven spoke. "First of all, a cul-ture is just the collective beliefs of a group of people. If you can change the *individual* beliefs, then yes, you can make an impact in the culture. But I want to make something very clear, Chris-tians don't *impose* their beliefs on anyone. We *propose* our beliefs to them. It ultimately comes to a quest for truth. Unfortunately, because so many people have filled every moment of their lives with entertainment or work, they leave no time to reflect upon the truly important questions—questions about ultimate truth. They've become so easily bored by overstimulation, they don't have the patience or the attention span to think about what matters most in life."

"No offense, but you sound like a preacher," Gunther stated with a sly grin.

"Maybe that's because he is," Braedon said.

"Really?" Gunther asked in surprise. "But I mean, he seemed so comfortable with a gun, and Braedon called you a master sergeant, like you were in the military. Then again, I suppose that just goes along with being a … being in the type of organization you're in."

"You mean, being a religious zealot?" Steven clarified.

"Well, I didn't mean…," Gunther stumbled over his words.

Steven smiled and held up a hand to put Gunther at ease. "No offense taken. Actually, I was a top trainer for the Elysium militia until, well, until I decided I'd had enough of their agenda. After that, I made a decision to spend the rest of my life helping others and doing what I could to further the kingdom of God."

Gunther frowned. "I don't know. Maybe I missed it somewhere, but how does fighting against the government have anything to do with religion? After all, aren't religion and politics two completely separate issues? What do archaic beliefs have to do with the issues facing modern times?"

"My friend, just because beliefs are ancient doesn't mean they aren't true. In fact, there are some truths that are *too* important to be new," Steven explained. "Many of the problems facing us today are due to the philosophy that religion and politics shouldn't intersect. Every decision a person and a government make is based on the worldview of that person or institution."

"I take it that when you say 'worldview' you mean how one views the world, right?" Gunther asked.

"Basically," Braedon interjected. "It's a set of underlying beliefs and principles that help form how you view reality."

"But it's deeper than that. It's your entire belief system," Steven summarized. "Every decision you make stems from your worldview. Let me give you an example. Do you believe it's wrong to murder someone in cold blood?"

"Of course," Gunther stated emphatically. "Murder is wrong."

"But why? What makes murder wrong?"

Gunther thought for a moment before answering. "I guess I would say because the majority of people agree it's wrong."

"So if I convince a majority of people it's okay to murder someone, would it then become right?" Steven asked.

Gunther shifted in his chair and shrugged. "I guess so."

"Do you really believe that?" Steven asked pointedly. "Let me ask you another question: do you believe man evolved over millions of years from a single-celled organism?"

"Yes," Gunther stated. "That *is* the prevailing scientific explanation for the origin of life. But how does this relate to a worldview?"

Steven gestured articulately with his hands as he explained. "Just this: you say murder is wrong, but your worldview contradicts your own beliefs. Based on your own words, I would propose that evolution is your underlying belief system or your worldview. So when someone asks if murder is wrong, you have to compare that to your belief in evolution. Following logic, if evolution is true, then we live by the rule of survival of the fittest. Therefore, if I want to murder someone, it shows I'm better able to survive than the other. Why would that be wrong?"

"But we're more evolved than that," Gunther countered. "We've developed social structures and guiding principles for behavior."

"Okay, but if social structures are just man-made, then men can change them whenever they want," Steven replied.

Gunther remained silent for several seconds. Braedon could almost see the gears turning in his brain as he processed Steven's argument. "I understand what you mean now by a worldview," Gunther said at last. "If I follow your logic, you believe your Christian worldview—namely that God created everything— should form your beliefs about how people should run their lives and how government should work. Is that correct?"

Steven smiled broadly. "Exactly. You see, Gunther, Christianity is more than just a religion. It's a truth claim about what's real. And if that truth is correct, then we should order *every* aspect of our life in line with that truth."

"But what if it isn't real?" Gunther asked.

"That's the very reason we shouldn't be so busy and distracted by entertainment," Braedon said. "For if we are, we won't have time to answer these questions."

"Gunther, let me be blunt with you," Steven said, suddenly serious. "We are all wanted men. And if Mathison and his Guardians catch us, we'll likely be killed. So let me ask you: what do you believe is going to happen to you when you die?"

"I'll cease to exist." Although Gunther made the statement casually, Braedon noticed he was wringing his hands together in his lap.

"How do you know?" Steven asked.

Gunther shrugged. "Because I believe in evolution, I guess."

"And why do you believe in evolution?"

"Because that's what the scientific majority believes."

"But have you researched it for yourself?" Steven asked.

"Somewhat," Gunther replied. "I've read articles and textbooks about it."

Steven rose to his feet, stepped over to a cabinet, and opened it. He withdrew a pistol and pointed it at Gunther. Startled, the scientist tried to move his body out of the line of fire.

"Don't worry, this gun's energy clip is empty," Steven said reassuringly. "See for yourself." He tossed the pistol to Gunther, who caught it nervously. He checked the power readings on the side of the weapon then handed it back to Steven.

"What was that all about?" Gunther asked, perturbed. "Why did you point an empty gun at me?"

"Would you give me permission to pull the trigger on a gun pointed directly at you, even after I told you it was empty?"

"No. I don't want you pointing that thing at me even if it's empty," Gunther stated. "You never know."

"Okay, so what you're saying is you'd want to investigate for yourself before putting your life in danger, and even then, you wouldn't want to take the risk," Steven confirmed. "Then why would you do that with your eternal soul? Why wouldn't you do your own research about what awaits you after death? Why do you just trust what others tell you when your *eternal* destiny is at stake?"

Gunther stood and looked at the other two men. "Listen, you've both given me plenty to think about, and I want to thank you once again for saving my life. But it's been a long day. If you'd be so kind as to point me in the right direction, I'd like to get some sleep."

Steven stood and looked at Gunther with genuine concern. "Sure. Your room's upstairs. Follow me."

The thought of sleep sent a sudden wave of weariness through Braedon's body. He yawned and stood as well.

Steven led the way up the steps. When they reached the top, he turned to look at Gunther. "Please, Gunther, understand that saving your life is just the beginning. The stakes are even higher than you're willing to admit. We *do* believe there's a God and that you have an eternal soul. You can deny the existence of gravity all you want, but if you jump out a window, you'll still have to face its effects. So we beg you to consider the claims of the Bible. Jesus really was God, and he paid the penalty for our sins. If you ask for forgiveness, He'll wipe them away and grant you eternal life with Him in heaven. Don't pass up this chance. None of us knows when we'll take our final breath."

Gunther smiled weakly as Steven stopped just outside the bedroom door. "Thank you for your concern. I'll think about what you've said. Have a good night." With that, Gunther entered his room and shut the door behind him.

Braedon gave his mentor a sideways glance as they continued down the hall toward their own rooms. "Things are moving faster than we had anticipated. If Gunther's right, Mathison could turn us all into his personal zombies at any moment."

"Today's events are just the beginning," Steven replied. "The time of planning and waiting has passed. Life in all of Tartarus is about to change radically."

16

THE VISITOR

"All finished," Braedon announced to Steven as he entered the kitchen area. The house was of average size and consisted of a single floor plus the finished basement. The kitchen was rather small, but the dining area next to it made it seem larger. The morning light streamed in through the closed curtains in the living room, illuminating the plain tan furniture that had clearly seen better days.

Braedon awoke early from a restless night of sleep. Steven had awakened shortly after. As the first order of business, Braedon took Gunther's data stick and made two copies of it. He handed one to Steven and placed the other into a zippered pocket on the side of his pant leg.

"Did you get a chance to sift through any of it?"

"Yeah," Braedon said, stifling a yawn. "While I was making the second copy, I skimmed it to get an overview. It seems legit. It'll take us weeks to go through all the data. And most of it's extremely technical."

"So our 'guest' was telling the truth. Not that I had any doubts. But now we've got to decide what to do with it. As much as I hate to wake Gunther so early, it can't be helped."

Steven left the kitchen and headed toward the guest room. A moment later, Braedon heard him knock on Gunther's door. Steven's voice echoed down the hallway. "Sorry to wake you, but it's almost six o'clock. We need to decide our course of action, and we should probably get moving before the Globe reaches full light output."

"All right. I'll be out in a moment," came the muffled reply.

Steven returned to the kitchen moments later and started a pot of coffee. It had just finished brewing when Gunther entered the room.

"Good morning," he said sluggishly. "That smells delicious."

Braedon and Steven returned the greeting. Steven poured a cup of coffee for each of them and handed them out. "The creamer is in the fridge and the sugar is on the counter."

"Black will be just fine," Gunther said before taking a sip of the steaming beverage.

With coffee mugs in hand, Steven led them into the living room area. Steven sat in a wooden chair, leaving the couch for Braedon and Gunther. Once they were seated, he began. "Braedon and I think it would be best if we got an early start this morning. We don't want to stay in one place for too long. With that in mind, we need to decide our next step. You indicated you could stabilize the portals. How? What do you need to make that happen?"

Gunther hesitated a moment before answering, "As I mentioned last night, I was hoping to find the prototype of the Portal Stabilizer, but I didn't. So Plan B was to download the research notes so I could build another one. Which, come to think of it, you should still have the data stick in your pocket. May I have it back?"

"Sure," Braedon replied. He withdrew Gunther's original stick and handed it to him.

Gunther took the offered device from Braedon, examined it quickly for damage, then tucked it into his pants' pocket. "The information on this drive represents years of work. With it, I should be able to reconstruct another prototype within—I don't know—six months, if I can get the materials and tools I need."

"Six months?" Braedon echoed. He glanced at Steven. "It looks like you were right. We'll have to find another location." Turning back to Gunther, he asked, "And what about materials? I'm assuming we're going to have to get some sophisticated stuff for you to build that thing."

Steven cut in. "We can worry about materials later. First things first. We can't stay in Elysium. We've got enough connections in the rest of Tartarus, so we should be able to get what we need. We'll just have to pray Mathison doesn't attack Bab al-Jihad before we can get the prototype built. If he does, it'll likely drag all of Tartarus into the conflict, making it nearly impossible for us to get what we need."

Braedon frowned. "Gunther, last night you said you could convert the Vortex weapon. Would that be a quicker option?"

"It's possible. Unfortunately, I haven't had time to look over the data I downloaded to even determine if that's feasible, or how long it would take to do so."

"We need to buy ourselves some more time," Steven stated. "So the question is, where do we go?"

"What about Cameron's group?" Braedon replied. "He's got enough extra space, and since he's their base is only a few miles from New China, we'd be able to get the parts we need easily enough."

Steven seemed to consider the idea before shaking his head in dismissal. "It's too far away. We need something closer."

Braedon and Gunther spent the next several minutes debating the pros and cons of each Crimson Liberty location. Gunther suddenly interrupted by clearing his throat loudly.

"What about Dehali?" he asked. "Travis is there. With his help, I could complete the prototype much quicker."

Steven's brow furrowed as he considered the suggestion. "We do know a couple of people in Dehali who are sympathetic to our cause, but their facilities are not nearly as secure as our other locations."

"I could really use his help," Gunther reiterated. "Together I'm sure we could—"

A loud crash coming from somewhere outside the house cut off the remainder of Gunther's sentence. The three men froze. When a second scuffling sound and thud were heard, Braedon leapt from the couch and ducked behind it, waving for Gunther to do the same. Steven joined them.

Braedon withdrew his laser pistol from its holster. Next to him, Steven's eyes lost their focus and the pinprick of light appeared on his temple. After several seconds, his focus returned and his body relaxed.

"What is it? What's goin' on?" Gunther asked.

Steven stood. "False alarm. I used my implant to check the camera feed. We've got an unexpected visitor."

Braedon relaxed at his mentor's assurance. He returned his gun to its holster and stood as well.

"A visitor?" Gunther asked in confusion and he rose to his feet. "How is that a false alarm? What kind of visitor? Are we in any danger?"

"It's a Box addict, or someone who is drunk. He stumbled onto our front step."

Braedon held up a reassuring hand. "It's nothing to be worried about. We're not in the nicest part of the city, so from time to time, we get stragglers, vagabonds, or addicts that show up on our doorstep."

"It's one of the reasons Crimson Liberty owns this house," Steven explained. "You see, Gunther, we're much more than just an organization dedicated to speaking out against tyranny. As we mentioned, one of our primary objectives is to fight for the sanctity of life—that means *all* life. If we didn't try to help people, our rhetoric would be hollow and meaningless."

"So what're you saying?" Gunther asked. "Are you suggesting you want to let him in and help him? I don't think that's a good idea. He might be crazy or something. He might rob us or … or worse."

Steven shook his head. "I don't think so. The way he's been acting and carrying on, it looks like he's suffering from the aftereffects of a night of marathon Box sessions. Don't worry, Gunther. We've helped many people like this man before. First, we'll wait to see if he snaps out of it and heads home by himself. If he doesn't, we'll bring him in, give him a little something to eat with some coffee, and see if that works. If not, then we'd normally take him to a rehabilitation center. However, under the present circumstances, we'll just have to alert some of the other members of Crimson Liberty and have them come over to take care of him."

Braedon felt the weight of their current situation settle in the pit of his stomach. He activated his implant and reached out to Steven. *I'm not sure this is a good idea. We've got enough to worry about right now. I think God would excuse us for not helping a man just this once.*

Braedon, I'm not going to leave him vulnerable to being robbed or beaten just because I'm busy, Steven countered. He ended the private conversation and spoke. "We need to eat and get ready to leave. This man isn't going to slow us down."

"I still think this is a mistake," Braedon stated.

"You know my philosophy," Steven said with a lighthearted smile. "If you're going to err, err on the side of compassion. If you get burned for your generosity, then rest assured your reward in heaven will be even greater. If we get caught because we helped a lost soul, God will take care of us. Trust Him with the outcome."

Steven headed to the front door to check on their visitor. Braedon stood silent for a moment, lost in his thoughts. Gunther walked up to stand next to him, a frown creasing his brow. "He is definitely a preacher. If it's any consolation, I agree with you. We've got more important things to do besides babysit some low-life. And what if this one addict causes us to fail in our plans and costs the lives of millions? Has Steven thought of that?"

Braedon shook his head in disagreement. "No. He's right. A single human life made in the image of God is more important than anything. Jesus said the good shepherd would leave the ninety-nine to help one lost sheep. If we only help others when it's convenient, then we undermine everything we stand for."

"Well, even if you guys aren't 'terrorists,' you are religious zealots," Gunther said, his tone carrying a hint of derision.

Although a sharp reply sprang immediately into his mind, Braedon decided to let the comment slide. He walked toward the front door with Gunther following behind.

Steven was already coming back into the house through the open door. He was supporting a young man who seemed clearly out of touch with reality. The visitor looked to be in his mid-twenties and was a couple inches shorter than Steven. His medium-length, wavy, dark hair was unkempt. His strong jaw sported a five-o'clock shadow with matching mustache, and his secondhand clothes were wrinkled and disheveled. Had he been better dressed, his hair combed and his face clean-shaven, he would have been quite handsome.

Once they were inside, Braedon closed the door and reached out to help Steven. The man suddenly pulled away and fell sideways onto the coffee table in front of the couch. The visitor looked up at the three men from atop the table and started waving his left hand at them as if trying to shoo them away.

"No…no, that's not right," the man murmured. "Computer, return to the Main Menu. Computer…computer!"

Steven helped him onto the nearby couch. "Can you hear me? Sir, what's your name?"

The man studied Steven for a moment, a confused look on his face. "Wait a second, this isn't the way the Intrepid looks. Computer, end program. Return to the Main Menu."

"Sir, what is your name?" Steven tried again. "Can you hear me?"

"Be careful how you address me, soldier," the man replied. "Don't you know who I am?"

"No, sir," Steven said. "Who are you?"

"I'm General Cornelius. I'm in charge of the fleet. Now release me and tell me what you've done with the ambassador. I need to speak to him immediately!"

"Pardon me, General Cornelius. We've been sent to see to your needs. Just lay down here on the couch and let me bring you something to eat." Steven nodded toward Braedon.

Recognizing the other's unspoken request, Braedon headed into the kitchen to prepare some food. He grabbed eggs and bread from the refrigerator. As he was placing two slices of bread into the toaster, Gunther entered.

"I have to admit, I'm amazed at Steven's patience," he said. "If it were me, I would've taken extreme pleasure in throwing the man into the street by his ear, not catering to him. We're wasting time!"

Braedon continued preparing the breakfast as he replied. "It'll only take a few minutes. Then we'll be on our way. Besides, I'm not just making breakfast for our visitor. I'm making enough for all of us."

Within a couple of minutes, Steven had the man settled onto the couch and came into the kitchen to grab a plate of food for their guest. Braedon finished serving the rest of the food and sat at the table next to Gunther. They had just begun to eat when Steven returned and sat next to them.

"He's resting now. Maybe he'll be better off when he wakes up. I've contacted the others. They'll send someone over to help him."

"At least you tried," Braedon commented.

"Yeah," Steven said distractedly as he took a bite of food. "The funny thing is he looks familiar to me. I think I may have seen him bef—"

The only warning the three men received was the clicking of the side door lock as it popped open.

Three people burst into the house, two from the side door leading into the kitchen and one from the front door. The first was a burly man with long blond hair hanging down past his shoulders. He rushed into the kitchen and grabbed Steven, who was closest to the door, and lifted him out of his chair. Following instantly behind the man was a thin woman of Asian descent.

Braedon's years of training kicked in. He pushed himself back from the table and drew his pistol. However, before he could point it at a target, the woman kicked it and sent it flying from his grasp. He struck out at the woman with a series of punches, which were limited by the cramped space of the dining area of the kitchen. His opponent smiled broadly as she easily blocked each attack. Stunned by her speed and grace, Braedon realized he was outmatched. It took all his concentration just to defend against her flurry of attacks. A handful of heartbeats later, his defense slipped. She landed a kick against his chest and sent him crashing to the floor.

Through a haze of pain, Braedon saw Gunther attempt to flee toward the front door. However, he had barely reached the threshold when a third person grabbed him and spun him around. The man pressed the barrel of a pistol against Gunther's temple.

"Don't move, any of you," he said in a commanding voice.

Braedon was surprised to see none of the intruders were dressed in anything resembling military or police uniforms. Instead, they wore plain street clothes. His surprise was deepened as he noticed the man with the gun was Arabic.

The large man holding Steven dropped him unceremoniously into one of the kitchen chairs and stood alert behind him. Steven looked up at the Arabic man and their eyes locked. Both of their expressions shifted to recognition and shock.

"Well, well, well," the man said in amusement. "This is quite an unexpected surprise. It's so nice to see you again, master!"

17

RAPTOR

Silence settled over the room as the two men stared at each other. After several moments, Steven spoke, "It's good to see you too, Rahib. And I honestly mean that, despite the circumstances."

The man's face hardened almost imperceptibly, causing a muscle in his cheek to twitch. "I don't go by that name anymore. My name is Raptor."

He had an Arabic accent, and the dark skin and features common to that culture. Yet his hair was trimmed in a style more common to modern Elysium. Braedon guessed he was about thirty years old, and, like his two accomplices, he was in excellent physical shape. His silky black dress shirt and pencil-thin mustache and goatee made his handsome face all the more striking. His overall appearance seemed more suited for a business office.

"A new name won't change your present or your past," Steven countered.

Raptor ignored the comment and pushed Gunther toward the table. "Sit."

As Gunther obeyed, Raptor turned toward the Asian woman. "Jade, help that one into his chair. There's no reason why we can't be more civilized."

The woman stooped and grabbed Braedon's arm. He winced in pain as she helped him stand. He stumbled toward the nearest chair and collapsed into it.

"Charon, make sure the area's secure," Raptor said. The big man strode toward the living room and nearly collided with another man who was just stepping into the kitchen.

"Whoa! You almost ran me over! Watch out for us little folk huh?" Braedon felt his heart sink as he recognized the newcomer.

"Move it or lose it," Charon said as he brushed past the man. "And go comb your hair. You look like a freak!"

The visitor smiled as he moved into the kitchen. He grabbed a slice of toast from Braedon's plate and began eating as he leaned against the wall. "Thank you, gentlemen, for the breakfast. The eggs were particularly delicious."

Steven frowned in disgust. "So it *was* an act after all. How noble of you to use a man's compassion against him."

"Hey, it ain't nothing personal," the former vagabond countered. "It just seemed like the most efficient way to gain entry. We'd heard you Crimson Liberty types were a bit soft when it comes to lowlifes, so we thought we'd see if it was true. Actually, you helped me win a little wager with Jade. She didn't think I'd even succeed in getting inside, much less be able to get our remote to figure out the door lock combination in time."

"Shut up, Traverse," the Asian woman said snidely, though her slight grin contrasted with her harsh words.

"Traverse?" Steven echoed. His expression changed as recognition dawned. "Xavier Traverse, the former actor turned con artist. I thought you looked familiar."

"Former?" he replied with a raised eyebrow, clearly affronted. "After such a successful performance?"

Steven ignored the comment and turned his attention back to the leader of the group. "So, Rahib," he began—Braedon smirked at the deliberate refusal to use the man's code name—"what misfortune have you encountered that you've been forced to surround yourself with such colorful characters?"

The Arabic man smiled and leaned toward Steven. "I could ask you the same question. In addition, I would add, 'What would cause a disgraced ex-soldier to break into a government compound and steal data and a weapon? Tell me, preacher, isn't it against your religion to steal?"

Steven didn't back down. "If you want to talk about religion, I'm all for that. But somehow, I don't think you really want to hear my answer. How did you know about the weapon, and what's in this for you? I can guarantee Crimson Liberty would be willing to make a counter offer."

Raptor leaned back as he ran his fingers across the surface of the gun. "Xavier here happened to be at the right place at the right time. Your little spat with the Cyborg was quite spectacular from what I hear. And although the invisibility cloaks are very effective against the casual observer, well, Xavier *isn't* a casual observer."

"What can I say?" Xavier shrugged. "I'm gifted."

"As for the purpose of your little duel, that wasn't hard to piece together if you know how to read between the lines of the unofficial government transmissions," Raptor continued. "Actually, our meeting is quite fortuitous. We've recently had a falling out with a powerful individual. The bounty we'll receive from turning you in should go a long way in making amends. Your two friends here have become quite famous, in case you haven't heard. Your pictures have been transmitted to all implant customers and personal handheld devices. Everyone in Elysium knows what you look like by now."

"Raptor, there's more at stake here than you know. Crimson Liberty may not be able to match the cash the government could give, but we can make up for it in other ways."

Raptor smiled. "I doubt it. You're not exactly the most popular or powerful group around."

Steven leaned forward. "Listen. I don't know what you've been told, but I need you to hear me out. Can we…can I talk to you alone?"

The Arabic man's eyes narrowed as he considered the request. "Fine. Jade, Xavier, watch these two."

"Sure thing," Xavier said cheerfully. "Then again, this one doesn't look like he's going to be much trouble anytime soon," he commented as he sat down near Braedon. "What did you do to him, Jade?"

Braedon ignored the comment. He watched the two men depart, hoping Steven would be able to somehow reason with the mercenary.

The conversation in the kitchen faded into the background as Steven led Raptor to the basement. When they reached the bottom of the stairs, Raptor paused, the gun still pointed at Steven's back. "Do I have your word you won't try to escape during our little 'chat'?"

"Yes, you can trust me," Steven said.

"Huh. Trust. That's interesting, coming from a man who lied to his family and all those who looked up to him," Raptor said with venom in his voice.

Steven continued to look straight at the younger man, his face impassive. "I know that's what you've heard, but it isn't true."

"Oh really? Then please enlighten me," Raptor said sarcastically.

Steven sat on the couch and closed his eyes a moment before speaking, "Look, Rah ... Raptor. It seems you've already made up your mind about me, and I don't know if anything I say will change that. However, I promise by everything I hold dear in this world what I'm about to tell you is absolutely true."

Raptor sat opposite Steven and began playing with his goatee, his expression hard. Steven looked calmly at his companion as he began speaking, "I'm sure by now you of all people have seen the corruption at the core of the Mathison administration. He and his people think they're above the law and that what they're doing is creating a more perfect world. And they'll stop at nothing to achieve their goals. Well, I got in the way."

"Of course you did."

Despite the pain the memory caused, Steven related to Raptor how he had been framed, how Mathison's people had defamed him and turned his family against him.

When he finished, Raptor remained silent for a moment as he considered the story. "You expect me to believe a man with your experience and intelligence fell so easily into that trap? Am I to believe you didn't at least prepare your family for what could come if you spoke out? C'mon. Don't insult my intelligence. Do you take me for a fool?"

"Of course not," Steven retaliated, his voice rising slightly in agitation. "But you know as well as I do how proficient Mathison is at twisting the truth. I *did* warn my family! But Mathison's people managed to make it look like I knew the truth was going to come out, and I was trying to cover my tracks. They certainly did their homework. They dug up some things from my wife's pain-filled past and played off of her innate fears. They did a masterful job of manipulating events."

Raptor narrowed his eyes at his former master, and for a heart-beat, Steven thought his chance of convincing the man of his innocence had been lost. Then, to his relief, Raptor relaxed slightly. "Five years ago I don't think I would've believed you no matter what excuse you came up with," he said. "But you're right. Since then, I've seen firsthand what Mathison is capable of."

Steven breathed in relief, then pressed the point. "Which is why it's so urgent you listen to me now. I don't know what you've been doing since that night you left ten years ago. But during the six years you were under my teaching, I saw potential in you. You're intelligent, a quick thinker, and you have a sharp mind. But you also carried a heavy burden of pain buried deep inside. Just when I felt you start to trust me and open up, you left."

"Well, what did you expect me to do after I'd just killed a man for messing with my girl? Stick around for tea?" Raptor remarked snidely.

"I'm not here to judge you for what you did. But you can't let your past determine your future."

"Where are you going with this?" Raptor asked, his impatience growing.

"I need your help," Steven implored. "This whole thing with the Vortex weapon is bigger than you. It's bigger than all of us! It's definitely bigger than any payoff you might receive for turning us in. I'm not exaggerating when I say that every person in Tartarus is going to be affected one way or another. And as things stand right now, you'll be the one to determine the course of events."

"C'mon, Steven, you don't have to sound so dramatic," Raptor replied. "What's so important about this weapon anyway?"

"The Vortex is just a part of it," Steven explained. "Mathison knows the leaders of Bab al-Jihad are gathering their strength to attack, so he's begun building an army. He believes the Guardians—and from what we understand, the Vortex—will give him an additional edge. But Mathison's also planning on using the Pandora's Box implants to control the minds of the citizens of Elysium! He's going to turn everyone in the city with implants into soldiers!"

Steven prayed silently as Raptor digested the news. "I knew he was crazy, but even I didn't expect this," Raptor said at last. He reached with his right hand to touch the spot where his own implant was housed. He swore, a look of disgust on his face. "That could be a problem, considering that I and everyone I know has that blasted implant! I'm not going to just sit around and allow myself to become someone's puppet. I want to see that data you retrieved."

"Sure."

"Your story makes sense of some other facts," Raptor said. "Mathison has had several of the criminal bosses on his payroll doing odd jobs for the past couple of years. I've even worked for him a few times. But none of us really understood what he was trying to accomplish. We just did our jobs and didn't ask questions.

"Now I understand," he continued. "Sometimes he sent us after information. Other times, it was technology or materials, and yet, other times, it was people—scientists mostly, all of which he was using to develop the Pandora's Box implants and the Vortex weapon."

"But there's even more to it than that," Steven said. "The elderly gentleman upstairs is a particle physicist who used to work for the government. It was his research Mathison used to make the Vortex. But that wasn't its original purpose. It was designed to stabilize the portals. With the data he stole from the compound last night, Gunther believes he can modify the Vortex weapon so it will make the portals go both directions! We can leave Tartarus and return to Earth!"

Raptor's skepticism was blatant. "They've been trying to find a way back for over two hundred years. I won't believe it 'till I see it."

"You don't have to take my word for it. Look at the data yourself."

"I intend to," Raptor replied.

"Do you see now why we need your help?" Steven asked. "You *can't* turn us in to the government. If you do, Mathison will win. You and your friends will become living robots for an egomaniac, and no one will ever know the way back to Earth was ever discovered. But if you help us, we can stop Mathison by opening the portals. And once we're on Earth, everyone will have a new beginning, a clean slate."

Raptor stood, walked over to a bookshelf, and began staring blankly at its contents. "A clean slate, huh?" he said softly. "Even being on Earth won't wipe away the past. It'll always remain. No. Earth is a chance for a new life, not a clean slate."

Steven rose and moved behind Raptor. Placing a hand on his shoulder, he said, "Rahib, I never did find out what caused you to leave home when you were so young, and honestly, I don't need to know. But God knows. If you would only—"

Raptor spun and knocked Steven's hand away. "Don't talk to me about your God!" he spat. "He's part of the problem!"

Shocked by his companion's vehemence, Steven took a step back. "I…I didn't mean to offend you. But if you tell me what happened, maybe I could—"

"No," Raptor said, more calmly. "Getting into a religious discussion with you is the *last* thing I want to do."

"That may be true, but figuring out what you believe is the most important topic a person could discuss," Steven replied. "Each religion makes a truth claim that needs to be examined like a jury trying to decide a court case. You have to examine the evidence, listen to the witnesses and see which one has the strongest argument."

Steven calmly endured the tirade, then looked at Raptor with a mixture of pity and sadness. "Raptor, I wish God would use someone else to speak to you. Since you've refused to accept His words, He will give you two signs."

Raptor narrowed his eyes and pushed Steven away from him. "We're done with this conversation. Get moving. We're going back upstairs."

"The first sign has already been given to you in the form of a dream," Steven said, his voice low and somber. "In it, you are walking through dark caverns being chased by an unknown creature. But in one particular cave, there is a sword."

To Steven's own ears, the words sounded foolish. But as he spoke, he saw Raptor's face grow pale. He could see that for the first time, real fear had gripped the other man. Steven took a deep breath and continued. "This dream has plagued you now for some time and will continue to do so as a reminder of the truth until the end of your days.

"The second sign is yet to come. Before this day is finished, the Lord of Hosts will demonstrate His power to you by preserving your life."

Raptor took a hesitant step toward him, his brow creased with confusion. "How...how did you know about my dreams? I've only told..." His expression transformed once more into hatred. "Oh, I get it now. You somehow figured out how Mathison is going to use the Box implants and put dreams in my head. Or just maybe, you're working *for* Mathison! Maybe this is all some kind of elaborate plan concocted by those government wackos."

Steven's unbelief spilled over from his face into his voice, coloring his words. "How can you believe that? *I don't know anything about your past!* I don't even know what the beginning of the prophecy is referring to!"

"But others do," Raptor countered. "I don't know how you dug up that information, but it's really a sick joke."

"Listen, Rahi–Raptor," Steven said determinedly. "Believe what you want for now. But once the second sign appears, you will have to face the truth. God has spoken to you, and I implore you to listen to Him. You only have thirty-one days left to live! You can no longer run from the hard questions about life and what will happen when you die. You need to find answers before it's too late! And although the wording of the prophecy can be interpreted in more than one way, it seems the only chance you have of saving yourself is to open the 'doorway to a new life.' Don't you see? You have to open the portals back to Earth!"

Raptor shook his head. "There is no God. There's no cosmic, all-powerful being that created everything. No one knows what's going to happen when we die. There's no way anyone can know, since no one comes back from the grave to tell the rest of us. It's a one-way, mysterious trip everyone faces alone. And until I have to go down that road, I'm going to get as much pleasure out of this world as I can. I'm not going to live my life bound by some archaic laws and rules made up by power hungry men."

"But there *is* a way to know!" Steven argued. "There *are* ways to know for sure. Look"—he removed a small device from his pocket—"I was once like you. I didn't think there was any way a person could know what lies beyond death's door." Removing a small memory chip from the side of the device, he handed it to Raptor. "I did a lot of reading and research. This is my personal journal. I summarized my findings and copied down some key quotes. Over the past several years, I've organized them so they would make the most sense. Please, read it and seriously consider—"

"You're wasting your time," Raptor snarled, holding out the memory chip for Steven to take. "I'm not interested. Even *if* you could convince me there's a God, he's not the kind of God I want to serve. He's impotent and cruel and a poor manager of affairs here in Tartarus and, from what I hear, on Earth as well. I will *not* bow my knee to him or any other god."

If Raptor had anything more to say on the matter, it was cut off by the sound of heavy footsteps on the stairs. Turning toward the steps, Raptor and Steven saw the large form of Charon appear a moment later.

"Sorry to interrupt, but I thought you'd want to know we've detected quite a bit of activity coming from the police transmissions," he said, a hint of urgency in his voice. "It appears they're doing a sweep of the city, starting at the Research and Records compound and working their way out. At that rate, they'll be in this area in a few hours. It may be better if we move this little party of ours to one of our own bases on the outskirts of the city."

Raptor threw one last glance in Steven's direction, then nodded to Charon. "Fine. Pull the hovervan next to the house, then get these three into the back. Xavier and I will follow in the truck. And make sure you put an implant inhibitor on the troublemaker. We don't want him calling for help."

Charon slipped past Raptor and grabbed Steven by the arm. He shoved him toward the stairs, his expression filled with disdain. As he climbed the steps, Steven glanced over his shoulder one last time toward Raptor. He whispered a brief prayer of thanks as he saw the man place the chip containing the journal into his pocket.

18

TRUTH

Raptor sat in the passenger seat of the electric, wheeled pickup truck as Xavier drove. Behind them, the hovervan containing Jade, Charon, and their three captives followed. Once the group had turned onto the main road leading to their base, Raptor took out the mini storage drive he had taken from Gunther and plugged it into his portable holoscreen. The instant he touched the "on" button, the device projected a holographic screen the size of a standard sheet of paper. The image hovered three inches in front of the palm-sized unit. In less than ten seconds, the entire contents of the drive had been loaded into the reader. Less than a minute after that, the information had been transferred wirelessly into Raptor's own digital storage device implanted in his skull. He repeated the process for Steven's journal and, after a few more moments, put the storage devices back into his pants' pocket. He returned his attention to the holoscreen and began perusing the files Gunther had stolen from the government computer.

"What's all that stuff?" Xavier asked as he drove.

"Some data our guests took from the government," he said absentmindedly, his attention still fixed on the screen. "I'll fill you guys in when we get back to the shop." Xavier took the hint and didn't ask any more questions, allowing Raptor to focus his attention on the data.

For the next twenty minutes, Raptor scanned through the various files in order to confirm what he had been told. He skimmed the classified memos, then flipped through the various diagrams and charts. Satisfied that Steven and the others had been telling the truth, and confident he had a decent grasp of the rest of the content, he exited out of the files.

As he was about to turn off the device, he remembered Steven's journal. Out of curiosity, he opened the first entry and began to read.

To my sons, Steven, Jr. and Seth,

I know you've heard many terrible things about me and are ashamed to be called my sons. My prayer is you will read this journal and come to know that Christianity is true. Even more, I pray you will act upon that truth and accept the forgiveness only Jesus can provide. Secondly, my hope is that after reading my journal, you will come to realize I would never do the things the government and media have claimed. For if I had, it would undermine everything I stand for. It would contradict everything I believe.

I will try to keep these notes as easy to understand as possible and offer as many examples as I can. I love you both.

Your father

Truth

Before I get into what I believe, I need to lay a foundation and define a few terms. For starters, have you ever wondered what truth really is? Is truth absolute (true for all people, at all times, in all places), or is it relative (does it change based on circumstances)? In other words, does truth change from culture to culture? Is truth the same for those born two thousand years ago as it is for those born today?

According to the dictionary, truth is defined as "conformity with fact or reality." By its very definition, truth is "that which is real."

So can truth change with circumstances? Can something be true for one person but not for another? There is something called the Law of Non-contradiction. Don't let the name confuse you. It simply means something can't exist and not exist at the same time (of course, this assumes it is equal in all ways). To put it another way, truth can't contradict itself.

For example: I cannot be in Elysium and not be in Elysium at the same time in the same way, or I cannot be a man and not be a man simultaneously. Although this seems like a stupid point to make, in reality, this law is crucial in order to know anything. Without it, we couldn't reason or make any positive claim about anything in life or in the universe. Without this law, science itself wouldn't exist.

Now let's apply this to the idea of truth. Something can't be true (real) for one person and not true for another. If that were the case, then it wouldn't be real! Remember, truth, by definition, is what is real. But many people deny absolute truth even exists. I've heard people say, "There are no absolutes". But that statement contradicts itself! Do you see the logical fallacy? The statement "there are no absolutes" is an absolute statement itself! Therefore, it is self-refuting. Another thing I've heard often is, "All truth is relative. What's true for you may not be true for me." But when you think about it, what they're really saying is, "That makes sense to you and seems right to you but not to me." They aren't really using the term truth to mean "what is real."

Okay, so what's the point to all this mental gymnastics? Well, keeping in mind everything I've said so far, I want to try to answer another question and define another term. What is religion? Religion, in a nut-

shell, is a truth claim. It's a set of statements that seeks to define reality. In other words, it's a search for truth! Since there are many different religions, there are many different truth claims. Obviously, in places where the religions contradict one another, they both cannot be true (Law of Non-contradiction).

For example: religion is like a scientific hypothesis. Scientists develop a hypothesis to explain why chemicals react certain ways under certain conditions, then they design experiments to test whether their ideas match reality. In the same way, religions offer explanations for why and how the universe exists, how it functions, and how to fix it. When people follow a certain religion, they are basically saying they believe religion A better explains reality than religion B. Science seeks to explain the reality of the natural, and religion seeks to explain the reality of the supernatural.

This means in each area of doctrine (set of beliefs) for each religion, we need to question how that doctrine matches reality. After all, just because someone believes something doesn't mean it's true, right? Let me show you a few examples. Mormonism teaches there are many gods, and in fact, even you can become a god. But Christianity, Judaism, and Islam teach there is only one God. Islam teaches that Jesus was just a prophet; Jehovah's Witnesses say he was an angel; and Christianity says he is God. Hinduism and Buddhism teach that we will be reincarnated when we die, but Christianity, Judaism, and Islam say we do not. Regarding salvation, those who say that "all paths/religions lead to God" are in direct contradiction to those who state, "Jesus is the only way to salvation."

Either one doctrine is right (true) and the other is wrong (untrue), or both doctrines are false. They can't both be true because they are contradictory statements. This is not to say that all religions don't contain some truth. It just means they may be correct in some teachings but wrong in their doctrine. For example, most religions teach that murder is wrong, but that doesn't mean the doctrine of reincarnation is correct.

While most of the major religions agree on some moral teachings, they have completely opposite doctrines that cannot be reconciled. They do not accurately represent all of reality.

For example: In the equation four plus four, the correct answer (truth/reality) is eight. The answer ten is incorrect, but it's closer to the truth than an answer of one hundred. If Christianity is the truth, then Islam and Judaism, which are both monotheistic religions (religions that believe in one God), are closer to the truth in this one aspect or doctrine than Hinduism and Buddhism, which are polytheistic (belief in many gods).

Unfortunately, too many people live their entire lives without even realizing that they believe things that are contradictory. And often, their beliefs don't match their actions, which only goes to show that what is really true for them is what they act upon, not what they claim to believe.

For example: A man might say he believes that when he dies he will have to answer for anything bad he did in his life, but then, hours later, he commits the very acts he just said he will be held accountable for. If he really believed he would be held accountable, he would act on that belief by not doing evil things. The truth, then, is that he doesn't really believe he will be held accountable, or if he does really believe it, he doesn't believe it enough to turn his beliefs into action. So since each religion is a truth claim, it is the responsibility of every human to examine those truth claims to discover which one best matches reality, then conform his/her life to that truth.

We are very much like jurors in a court case. We must consider each hypothesis (religion) carefully, examine the evidence thoroughly, and base our conclusions on logic and research. If I reach the conclusion Islam is true, then I want to change my life and become the best Muslim I can. If I believe Buddhism is correct, then I want to be a great Buddhist. And if I come to the conclusion there is no God, then I will become a sincere atheist.

The single most important question a person can answer in life is, "What is going to happen to you when you die?" The way you answer this question will determine how you live and what actions you take.

For example: if evolution is true, then when I die, I will cease to exist. Therefore, I should seek as much pleasure in this life as possible. If Hinduism is true, then when I die, I will be reincarnated based on my works. Therefore, I should do good deeds to others so I can erase my bad karma. If Christianity is true, then when I die, I will face judgment, and only those who accepted Jesus' forgiveness will enter heaven. Therefore, I should accept his forgiveness and live my life according to his commands.

My sons, don't wait to do this research for yourself. Life is short. Because this issue is so important, I implore you to put all your effort into finding the answer. And it is my belief that if you do so, you will come to the same conclusion I have reached.

Raptor turned off the handheld device and put it back in his pocket. He hadn't meant to read the entire thing, but was surprised to find it so intriguing. He had heard people talk about religion and debate issues, but he had never read anything approaching the topic from a foundational perspective. Despite his own bias against Steven and his beliefs, Raptor couldn't stop his mind from mulling over the logic. *You're an atheist,* the voice in his head repeated.

Yeah, but only by default. I've never really looked into what the other religions teach and why they believe it. But that's because I don't believe there's a God. Maybe if I did, it would make sense to research things. Evolution has proven God isn't real. Everything came about by natural processes.

Yet no matter how hard he tried to push the nagging thought away, it kept returning. *Are you sure about that? Steven's right. The question of what will happen after you die is the most important question in life, but you've never given it much thought.*

"Hey, Raptor. Did you drink some bad juri juice or something?"

Xavier's words jolted Raptor out of his musings. "No, I'm fine. Why?"

"Oh, I don't know," Xavier replied. "It's just I've never seen you just stare into space for a minute without blinking before. At least, not without using your implant. The stuff on those data drives must be pretty heavy indeed for it to have that kind of effect on you."

Raptor winced. "Yeah, I guess you could say it's heavy." He paused for a second as he debated whether or not to say anything more. "Let me ask you something. You're a Christian, right?"

Xavier threw his boss a strange look before turning his attention back to the road. "Uh … sure. I guess you could call me that. But just for the record, I'm not one of those crazy fundamentalist types. I believe in God, go to church once in awhile, say my Hail Marys and go to confession. Why do you ask?"

Raptor ignored the question. "Do you believe Christianity is the truth and other religions are wrong?"

"Well, I wouldn't go that far," Xavier said as he cocked his head to the side and grimaced. "After all, who's to say Christians have the monopoly on truth. It seems to make sense to me that as long as you're sincere, God will let you in."

"But can't you be sincerely *wrong* about something?" Raptor asked.

"Okay, so I guess I should say you have to be sincere about doing good deeds."

"Such as?"

"I don't know—give to the poor, help other people, don't be selfish…stuff like that," Xavier stated.

"So basically, just follow the Ten Laws," Raptor said.

Xavier let out a boisterous laugh. "The Ten Commandments, not the Ten Laws!"

Raptor grinned despite his mistake. "Yeah, the Ten Laws just doesn't have the same ring to it. By the way, take Coney Avenue to the shop. I want to come in from the alley."

"Sure thing, boss," Xavier said as he turned onto the indicated street.

"Can you name any of them?" Raptor asked, resuming the conversation.

"What? The commandments?"

"Yeah."

Xavier thought for a moment before answering. "You shouldn't kill, you shouldn't lie, you shouldn't steal. What's that other one … oh yeah, you shouldn't cheat. I don't remember the rest off the top of my head."

"So do you keep the Ten Commandments?" Raptor asked.

The con man turned to stare at his employer. Based on the expression on his companion's face, Raptor could tell he wasn't very thrilled with the turn the conversation had taken. "Why the sudden interest in my beliefs?" Xavier asked, dodging the question.

Raptor shrugged. "Don't worry, it's not that big of a deal. I was just curious."

Xavier studied Raptor's expression a moment longer before finally answering. "Listen, I may not be the poster boy for Christianity, but I could be a lot worse. Take Charon's wacko brother, Marcel. I mean, I can understand the guy would get ticked off at us because we owe him ten-thousand dollars, but then he lies to us about the Nelson deal, cheats us out of our share, and kills poor Collins just because he felt like it. I think in the grand scheme of things, when compared to guys like Marcel, I've got nothing to worry about."

"Is that part of the church's teachings? As long as you're not as bad as other people, then you get into heaven?" Raptor asked. "Where do they draw the line? Is this teaching in the Bible?"

"Where is all this coming from?" Xavier replied, his expression one of complete confusion. "Who are you, and what did you do with Raptor?"

Laughing lightly, Raptor stretched and let out a sigh. "I don't know. It's just something Steven said that got me thinking. That's all."

"Steven? The big, bald, dark-skinned guy?"

Raptor nodded. "Yeah, that guy."

Xavier harrumphed. "I wouldn't take anything he says seriously. I mean, here's a guy who claims to be religious yet cheats on his wife and takes her money to boot. What a hypocrite."

Raptor didn't respond as Xavier brought the truck to a stop in front of their base. Raptor and his associates ran a marginally successful auto repair shop as a front to their criminal activities. The rectangular building housing the shop consisted of a fairly large front-office section, several internal rooms and storage areas. In addition, the main auto shop was located in the back of the building. It had two large garage doors leading into it, one at each end. At least, that's what was visible to the average customer. But beneath the shop, the group had built an extensive network of rooms and hallways which were used for a variety of nefarious purposes. The entire building was surrounded by an eight-foot high electromagnetic fence. Since it was still early in the morning, the normal business crowd and employees had still not arrived, leaving the place deserted.

Xavier gave a mental command via his wireless implant and the gate opened. He drove the vehicle into the back parking area, which contained a selection of hovercars and vans in various stages of repair. As they pulled into the lot, Raptor did his customary scan of the area to make sure nothing was out of the ordinary. Xavier pulled into one of the empty spaces near the back of the building while Jade parked the hovervan in front of a smaller entrance next to the southern garage door. Xavier sent another command to the gate, closing it.

Raptor used his implant to check the feeds from the cameras mounted on the fence. Satisfied the coast was clear, he gave Charon a mental command to move the prisoners into the building. The side door of the van immediately slid open. Charon herded the three blindfolded men out of the vehicle and through the side entrance.

Once the prisoners were secured in one of the secret rooms below the building, Raptor assembled his team in one of the upstairs offices. Jade entered last. A flying animal similar to a gray squirrel with leathery wings was perched on her shoulder.

"It's just past seven o'clock, so we've got to make this quick. I want us out of here before the morning crew arrives," Raptor said, his tone businesslike. "It turns out, we got more than we bargained for with our captives." Raptor related to the other three the conversation he had with Steven, as well as the information he gleaned from the stolen data. For now, he decided to leave out the details about the prophecy and signs. When he finished, he looked at each of them in turn. "Since this isn't a normal job situation, I'd like each of your opinions before we take a vote on how to proceed. Do we turn them in and take the money to pay back Marcel, or do we help these guys try to find a way to Earth?"

"I don't trust these religious fanatics," Charon said. "We have no guarantees anything they've said is true. They're probably lying about being able to stabilize the portals. Scientists have been trying to do that since the First Colony arrived in Tartarus. I say we turn 'em in, get our reward, and pay our debts."

Raptor studied Charon briefly, then nodded. "Anyone else?"

Jade crossed her arms, a defiant look on her face. "I don't think the government would be offering such a large amount for these men unless they stole something very important. If anything they said is true, we can't just turn them in. You said those documents looked legit, right?"

"Yes. Down to the governmental file numbers," Raptor confirmed.

"Then I say we trust 'em. I don't want to be turned into some walking zombie. And if there's a chance we can get out of Tartarus, I'm willing to do what I can to make that happen. I vote to help them."

All eyes turned toward Xavier, who held up his hands in surrender. "Look, I'm not sure what to think. Charon's got a point. I don't want his big bad brother to string me up for robbing him. But then again, I don't much like the idea of being a mindless zombie either. So I think I'll sit this one out."

"Well then, I guess you get to cast the deciding vote, O Illustrious Leader," Jade said, turning toward Raptor.

Steven's cryptic words came rushing back to him. *"The lives of thousands rest in your hands. Tens of thousands will live or perish by your choices."* Feeling the weight of the decision, Raptor paused and closed his eyes in an attempt to clear his mind. After several seconds, he opened them and faced the others. "I think we should—"

His words were cut off by a loud commanding voice coming through each of their wireless implants. ***This is Inspector Hawkins of the Elysium Security Force! We have the building surrounded! Release your hostages now!***

19

NEGOTIATIONS

Raptor and his companions exchanged looks of shock and confusion. "What!" Charon exclaimed angrily. "How did they find us?"

"I don't know," Raptor said in puzzlement.

"But I thought we had an agreement with Mathison's people," Jade commented. "Why would he send Hawkins after us now?" Sensing her master's agitation, her winged pet let out a series of clicks and chirps.

"It has to have something to do with our hostages," Xavier replied. "They probably knew they were somewhere in the vicinity, but we beat them to the punch and captured them first. They must've followed us here somehow."

"Maybe. Then again, not all of Mathison's people know we're on his payroll," Raptor said. "Whatever the case, we've got to figure out what to do about this. Let me see if I can get a little more info." He mentally switched on his implanted commlink and used the microphone embedded in his lip to convert his voice. "Inspector Hawkins, this is Mahmoud Salib," Raptor said, using one of his aliases. Putting just the right amount of uncertainty in his voice, he continued. "We...uh...we don't know what you're talking about. My associates and I were just preparing to open the shop for the day. We don't… we don't know anything about any hostages."

He didn't have to wait long for a reply. *Don't play dumb with me, Raptor. We know you're holding hostages. We've already got enough against you to put you away for the rest of your life. I don't think you want to add the murder of three innocents to that, do you? If you come along peacefully, you have my word your cooperation will be taken into consideration at your trial. Oh, by the way, don't even think of trying to sneak out through the 'secret' underground tunnel. We've got that covered as well.*

Raptor returned his voice to normal. "Well then, Inspector, it appears I don't have many options. Give me a couple of minutes to retrieve the hostages."

No! You get them out here now, or we come in after them! Hawkins shouted.

"No need to get trigger happy," Raptor replied. "We'll bring them out as soon as possible. They're locked in a room downstairs. It'll take us at least a minute to get down there, untie them, and get them back upstairs."

Fine. But if I get the slightest hint you're trying to pull something, we'll be on you before—

"Understood." Raptor said, cutting him off. He returned his attention to the others. "The ESF aren't here for our hostages. They're here because someone turned us in."

Charon swore violently. "Marcel!"

"Really?" Xavier asked in surprise. "What makes you so sure?"

"Several reasons," Raptor explained. "One, our dear inspector called Steven and his companions 'hostages' and said they were 'innocents.' If he was after them for stealing from the government, he would've called them criminals, fugitives, or some other nasty word. And he most *definitely* wouldn't have referred to them as innocents."

"Unless he's deliberately trying to throw us off," Jade countered.

"But if he was, then by doing so, he's giving us more power in the negotiations," Raptor replied. "The deaths of hostages are a lot worse for public relations than the death of a couple of fugitives. Second and most importantly, he knows about our underground tunnel. Only one of our associates in the criminal networks would know about that exit. And considering how Marcel feels about us right now, I think it makes the most sense he's the one who turned us in."

"Okay, so what do we do?" Xavier asked, his anxiety slipping through his normally calm demeanor.

"I'm not sure yet," Raptor said. "But I'm thinking we might be able to use the help of our 'hostages.' Charon, bring them up here."

"We don't need them," Charon protested. "Why don't we just turn ourselves in? You know Mathison will get us off the hook."

"Because if we do, we pretty much doom ourselves to becoming either slaves of Mathison, casualties in a war, or both!"

"So you've just bought into everything Russell said, huh? Just like that."

"I trust what my own eyes have seen," Raptor retorted. "The data on that drive is real. We don't have time to waste right now. Just go get them!" Raptor commanded. Charon cast one last frustrated look at his friend before exiting the room.

A heavy silence hung in the air for several seconds. Finally, Raptor spoke. "Let's focus on putting together a plan. Any ideas?"

Xavier hesitated just a moment longer before responding, "Well, we've got those invisibility cloaks. Could we somehow use those?"

Raptor shook his head. "Maybe. The problem is, those only work under poor lighting conditions, unless your only goal is to hide but not move. We'll have to keep that in mind, though.

"Can we just use one of the cars in the shop to escape?" Jade suggested.

"None of those are running right now," Raptor said.

"What about that new weapon or the Volt? Maybe we could use those?" Jade offered.

"I'm not sure we want to use that Vortex weapon," Raptor replied. "From what I've read, it seems like it might be unpredictable. But we'll definitely want to keep the Volt handy in case the ESF brought a Guardian with them. What we really need is to find out what we're up against in case it comes to a fight."

"Can't we just check the camera feeds?" Xavier asked.

"No. I already tried. The ESF have jammed them," Raptor replied.

"What about Zei?" Jade suggested, nudging the flying mammal on her shoulder. It cooed softly.

Raptor grinned at the idea. "Yes. Send him out through the skylight and have him circle around the building a few times."

Nodding, Jade slipped out the door of the room to go release her flying pet. Raptor withdrew his holoscreen and activated it. As the two men waited, they heard the sounds of approaching feet. Steven, Braedon, and Gunther entered, Charon following close behind. Their hands were no longer bound and their blindfolds had been removed.

Raptor launched into a summary of the situation. "Time is short, so listen carefully. It seems Charon's brother, Marcel, has turned us into the ESF. They have us surrounded, and our emergency exit is blocked. They want us to release our 'hostages', but they don't seem to realize exactly who it is we've captured."

"I'm sure they'll figure it out real quick if you do turn us over to them," Steven stated.

"Which is why we don't plan to," Raptor said. "I think it would be in all our best interest if we work together on this. Are you with us?"

Steven exchanged a brief glance with Braedon before responding. "Of course. What do you have in mind?"

Before Raptor could reply, Inspector Hawkin's voice came through his implant. *Time's up.*

The criminal leader glanced at each of the men assembled in the room. "I'm going to stall for time. Jade's releasing her mindim. As it flies around the outside of the shop, the microscopic camera embedded in its head will allow us to see what we're up against. Charon, get the satchel containing the Vortex weapon and Volt. We might need those." As Charon exited the room, Raptor turned to Xavier. "Take off their inhibitors," he said, motioning toward Braedon and Steven. As the con artist obeyed, Raptor finally replied to the ESF officer.

"Listen carefully, Inspector. You can have the hostages, but you're going to have to let me and my colleagues go. If you or any one of your men tries to play the hero, the evening holofeeds are going to be posting a story about how one of the precious ESF inspectors failed in his negotiations with known criminals. These kinds of things can be very damaging to an otherwise promising career."

Raptor paused to allow the threat to sink in. The holoscreen built into the nearby desk sprang to life with the images being transmitted from Jade's pet as it flew around the building. He studied them with interest even as he continued his conversation.

"Here's how this is going tso work: I'm going to release two of the hostages to you. One of my men will accompany them to the south garage door. You will then allow him to enter the hovervan parked there and drive it into the vehicle bay. We'll leave the third hostage tied up inside the shop. Once we're all aboard the van, you'll allow us to drive it out of the lot. When we're safely out of the city, you can go in to retrieve the third hostage. But just so you know, we're leaving a little package with the last hostage. If you try to attack us, you'll find pieces of this shop blown halfway to the governor's mansion. Got it, or do I need to repeat it for you?"

There was a long pause, making Raptor wonder if the man was going to go for it. Finally, the voice of the inspector returned, *Understood. You know this is just buying you a little time. We'll find you again.*

Raptor ignored the boasts and shut off his microphone transmitter.

"How is turning us over to the ESF going to help us?" Braedon challenged. "In case you don't remember, you said yourself everyone in Elysium will recognize Gunther and I! I don't think this inspector will—"

"Don't presume to tell me what to do!" Raptor interrupted, his anger barely restrained. "I know what I'm doing. Now if you'll shut up for a minute, I'll explain the plan."

Steven placed a calming hand on Braedon's shoulder. Braedon took in a deep breath. "Fine."

Raptor was used to hotheads like Charon taking hours to calm down. He was impressed by Braedon's self-control. It served to deflate his own irritation. "Based on the images from Jade's mindim, there's a dozen men stationed outside—four covering each of the two garage doors and another four covering the front and side office doors. We know the ESF got through the outside gate without raising any alarms, so they must have been given the codes, once more pointing to Marcel as their informant. That means they were waiting to ambush us, but didn't count on us having prisoners. This can work to our advantage. If we play our cards right, we can all avoid getting taken by the ESF."

Steven leaned in closer. "Okay. So what've you got in mind?"

Raptor gave his former mentor a lopsided grin. "Here's what we're going to do."

"Here they come," the officer standing next to the inspector said softly as the southern door of the shop opened.

It's about time, Inspector Jonathan Hawkins thought as the two hostages came into view. The inspector was not a particularly brilliant man. But like an expert gambler, he had a knack for being able to assess situations in order to figure out how to come out on top. Sometimes that meant bribing the right official at the right time, and sometimes it meant choosing the right side to be on in a fight. When he initially accepted this assignment, he thought his intuition had been misguided. But with the appearance of hostages, he knew instantly he had struck gold once more.

When most of his other colleagues had been assigned to look for the two fugitives, he had quickly volunteered to lead the force that would try to capture this small gang of criminals. He felt he'd have a better chance of getting his promotion if he could successfully bring in a gang, rather than wasting his time on some wild endek chase looking for fugitives who had probably fled the city. The arrest of the gang alone would have been impressive, but now, if he could bring in the gang *and* rescue three hostages, his promotion would be assured.

All he had to do was make sure everything went according to plan.

Lang and Haupt, move in and help the hostages, Hawkins commanded mentally. The men left their positions behind the hovercar resting thirty feet to the left of the Inspector's own vehicle and moved cautiously toward the two prisoners.

As they moved in, Hawkins could see their escort, Xavier Traverse, step away from the hostages and climb into the nearby hovervan as per the negotiated agreement. Hawkins leaned against the side of his car, his pistol tracking the man's movements. So far, everything seemed to be proceeding appropriately. The hovervan's engine rumbled to life as the garage door leading into the shop opened. The large mechanized door stopped with just enough room for the van to slip through. As Traverse pulled the vehicle inside the building, Hawkins scrutinized the interior, searching for any signs of attack or any clues that might prove useful. However, the light cast by the Globe, which hung low in the east, was unable to pierce the darkness of the southern-facing shop.

Once the van was enveloped by the shadows inside the building, Hawkins switched his attention to the two hostages his officers were now escorting back to the safety of the far side of the police vehicle. Both men looked ragged and weary, and their clothes and faces were stained with dirt and grime. The inspector wondered how long they had been held captive and under what conditions. Although the dark-skinned, older man looked strong for his age, his shoulders sagged, and he leaned heavily on his left leg, indicating an injury. The younger man's short, cropped hair, muscular build, and steady gait gave Hawkins the impression he had spent time in the military.

The inspector narrowed his eyes as the two officers returned to their position behind the car with the hostages. *Something looks familiar about that younger one,* he thought as he studied his features more closely. The truth struck him and his face lit up in shock. *The height! The hair! The build! It can't be!*

However, before Inspector Hawkins could form another coherent thought, chaos exploded around him.

Several laser blasts seemed to materialize out of thin air from somewhere near the garage opening. They struck the vehicle next to him, shattering the back window and causing shards of flying glass to embed themselves in his face and neck. Hawkins fell to the ground, reeling from the attack and the resulting pain. The deep cuts from the glass made his face feel as if it were on fire. He moved into a sitting position with his back against the car and glanced to his left. The unconscious body of his partner lay slumped over the hood.

Once his mind recovered from the initial shock, he activated his wireless commlink. *Officer down! We're taking fire at the south entrance! Lang and Haupt, watch out for the—.* His words died on his lips. Both officers lay unconscious on the ground. Their weapons were now in the hands of the former hostages and were pointed in his direction. Before he could warn the rest of his force, a bright flash erupted from one of the weapons. His world faded to black.

You've got two more officers coming toward your position around the east side of the building and another two coming from the west, Raptor warned. Braedon sent a quick acknowledgement back to the gang leader, then changed the frequency of his implant to communicate with the police force. *This is one of the hostages! Inspector Hawkins is down as are the other three officers! Please help us! We're hiding behind the police car nearest to the gate.*

Braedon rose just enough so he could see over the back of the vehicle. He waved quickly to the two approaching officers who were even now cautiously making their way to the edge of the building, their weapons at the ready.

Where are the attackers? one of the officers asked Braedon silently.

I'm not sure, came his mental reply. *I don't see anyone now. The coast looks clear.*

The first officer took up a position at the edge of the building and covered the area with his pistol. His partner sprinted toward the police vehicle. Once there, he knelt and checked on the fallen officers. Steven knocked him unconscious with a well-placed blow to his head. Braedon simultaneously stunned the other unsuspecting officer, dropping him to the ground with a single shot.

The other two officers came around the east side of the building just in time to see their comrades fall unconscious. Braedon ducked behind the car as laser blasts struck nearby. He waited a moment, then peered around the front bumper. The two officers were so focused on Braedon and Steven, they failed to notice the slight bending of light behind them. The nozzles of two weapons protruded from the edge of the invisibility cloaks. Jade and Charon opened fire on the surprised policemen, dropping them instantly.

The other two are down, Charon reported.

Great. That just leaves the two guarding the front door, Raptor replied. *With any luck, we'll be out of here before they can cause any problems. But just in case, Jade and Braedon, I want you to set up watch at the corners. We're almost finished loading, then we'll get out of here. Charon and Steven, come back inside and help us finish up.*

Braedon and Steven each sent a short acknowledgement. Braedon and Steven bolted back toward the shop. When they arrived, Braedon settled into position while Steven and Charon disappeared into the darkened interior.

A sudden explosion from within the building knocked Braedon and Jade off their feet. Stunned by the blast, Braedon shook his head to ward off the aftereffects of the shock. He stood slowly, using the wall for support. Jade was also back on her feet and sprinting toward the garage door from the opposite side.

Braedon reached the large opening seconds after the martial-arts expert. His eyes took a moment to adjust to the darkness.

When they did, he felt his stomach tighten in fear. The bodies of Steven and Charon lay unmoving on the debris-strewn floor several paces from the side of the hovervan. The vehicle's engine was still running and the sliding side door stood ajar.

But the source of his fear was a seven-foot tall, muscular being standing in the doorway leading to the offices. The figure had a massive claw around Raptor's throat and had lifted him several feet into the air. This was no ordinary soldier. It was a Type II Guardian. A hybrid!

20

THE SECOND SIGN

The genetically-altered soldier twisted his longer-than-average neck in the direction of the newcomers. Braedon had encountered specimens of each of the three types of Guardians before. Each time he had been both impressed and repulsed by the blending of human and animal traits in the Type II and Type III versions. The part-animal portion of this Guardian's DNA clearly came from a reptile. The man's face, while mostly human looking, had the slightly-elongated snout of a snake and was covered with dark-brown scales instead of skin. His muscular body was concealed by the black, skin tight armor worn by the Guardians, yet he had removed his helmet. Braedon had heard the Chimeras and Titans did this to shock and intimidate their opponents.

And based on Jade's expression, it was working.

The martial arts expert seemed rooted to the spot, her gaze held by the blood-red reptilian eyes staring back at her across the shop. The Guardian studied Jade and Braedon, his grotesque expression splitting into a grin. His forked tongue shot out of his mouth and moved rapidly over his razor-sharp teeth.

The hybrid tossed Raptor aside, sending him crashing to the ground near the van. The sudden movement served to awaken both Braedon and Jade from their stupor. They raised their weapons and opened fire. The Guardian leapt to the side with such speed Braedon lost sight of him.

"What the...where'd he go?" Jade asked.

The Guardian dove from the shadows and knocked the pistol out of Jade's hand. He immediately switched directions and rolled toward Braedon.

Braedon leapt backward and managed to fire several shots, two of which found their mark. However, whether due to the black armor or the man's own scaly skin, the shots seemed to have little effect. The Guardian came out of his roll and kicked out with his left leg, sweeping the feet out from under Braedon. The crash onto the grease-stained floor knocked the wind out of him.

Now weaponless, Jade threw off her invisibility cloak and let out a cry of fury. She launched into a series of punches and kicks that would have incapacitated a normal man. Yet despite her skill, Braedon knew she was no match for the Guardian. With a nearly two-foot height advantage and increased agility, the man was able to block most of the blows with ease. The ones that did manage to slip through his defenses merely served to aggravate him as they bounced harmlessly off his armor.

Braedon got back to his feet and joined in the melee, hoping his stronger frame and taller stance would serve to keep the man off balance. He felt his hopes rise as the Guardian backpedaled away from his two attackers. However, within seconds the reptilian hybrid went on the offensive. The man's powerful blows sent both his opponents reeling.

Jade lost her footing on the pebble-strewn floor and fell hard onto her left side. The Guardian sent a kick into her stomach, doubling her over in pain. With one attacker down, the genetically-enhanced soldier turned his full attention to Braedon. He launched into a series of powerful blows that knocked Braedon to the floor.

Braedon rolled to his side and scrambled to return to his feet. A kick landed against his side. A rush of agony tore through his body. The blow sent him tumbling.

Get up, Braedon! His will demanded. But his body protested. His vision cleared just in time to see the Guardian bearing down on him.

A small, winged creature flew into the reptilian face, its claws digging at his scaly hide. Caught off guard by the sudden assault from Jade's mindim, the Guardian stepped backward and crashed into one of the many racks of car parts and tools. He howled in pain as several of the heavy items fell on him. His arms flailed in an attempt to strike the annoying creature. The mindim broke off the attack and flew out of range, coming to rest on one of the overhead beams.

Jade, we have to find a weapon! Braedon called out to her mentally as he rose to his feet. *I'll try to hold him off while you—*

Before Braedon could finish the thought, the Guardian regained his balance. The half-human beast howled in rage and lunged toward his enemies.

Braedon tried desperately to dodge the attack. The Chimera's body slammed into his side. The momentum sent the two combatants flying several feet across the floor toward the center of the room. Braedon blacked out momentarily from the force of the blow. When he regained consciousness, he opened his eyes to see the grotesque reptilian face staring down at him. But to his surprise, the slit, red eyes suddenly filled with pain and fury. The Guardian rolled off Braedon and fell sideways to the ground.

Steven was clinging to the man's back. His arm was wrapped around the hybrid's neck in a choke hold. Using his larger size and greater strength to his advantage, the Guardian rolled until Steven was beneath him. He grabbed Steven's pinky finger tightly and pulled it backward. Steven cried in pain and released his hold. Braedon watched in horror as the Guardian leapt to his feet and lifted Steven into the air. He hurled him onto the hood of a nearby hovercar resting on a repair lift. The front windshield shattered with a loud crash as Steven's body slammed into it.

Braedon let out a feral cry as he forced his weary body to respond. Rising unsteadily to his feet, he grabbed a large wrench that had fallen to the floor near him and threw it at the Guardian. The man blocked the object with a swipe of his arm.

Raptor suddenly appeared behind the Guardian. He slammed a heavy, metal pipe into the back of the hybrid's legs. The blow should have broken the Guardian's bones, but merely made him stumble and fall to his knees. Raptor leapt forward and prepared for another strike. A laser blast suddenly shot across the room from the door on the north wall and struck his left arm. Raptor reeled from the impact and lost his grip on the metal bar.

Braedon turned his head in the direction of the attack. The last two police officers had entered the building. He searched frantically for signs of the others. Charon still lay unmoving near the southern door, and Jade was curled into a fetal position on the floor as she struggled to recover from the Guardian's kick. Xavier, who was in the driver's seat of the van parked near the eastern wall of the shop, was just beginning to stir.

It was over. They had lost.

The side door of the van suddenly slid sideways. Gunther stood inside the opening. In his hands was the Vortex weapon, which was pointed directly at the two police officers. His hands shook violently. The scientists braced himself against the frame and pulled the trigger.

Instead of the typical loud crack of a ballistic projectile or laser beam, the Vortex produced what sounded like a rushing wind. It emitted a narrow cone of particles that completely missed the intended targets and instead hit the northern wall of the shop between the two officers. Time seemed to freeze. The gazes of everyone in the room became fixated on the spiraling cone as it grew in size. The officers backed slowly away from the expanding circle of energy.

The ring of particles, which had reached almost four feet in diameter, exploded outward, knocking everyone off their feet. As Gunther fell, he released the trigger of the weapon, shutting off the continuous stream. Braedon stared in surprise and horror. The cone had disappeared, but the circle of particles remained.

They had transformed into a miniature black hole.

Everyone and everything in the room began to be pulled toward the swirling vortex. Braedon reached out and grabbed onto one of the vehicle support beams. The gravitational force slowly increased, straining his muscles.

The officers let out cries of terror as they were lifted off of their feet and flew toward the tear in space. When they reached the center, their bodies twisted and contorted unnaturally until they finally disintegrated and disappeared.

The Guardian, who had been standing in the center of the room, looked around frantically for something to grab. Catching sight of a grate in the floor used to collect spilled fluids, the reptilian hybrid leapt toward it. However, the pull of the vortex threw off his aim, and his gloved hands fell short of their mark. He clawed frantically at the smooth concrete. A growl of dread escaped from his throat as he was inexorably drawn closer and closer to the hole.

Letting out a final cry, the Guardian's body contorted as it too was torn apart by the gravitational forces.

Gunther wore an expression of revulsion and horror. He dove back into the interior of the hovervan and slammed the door. An engine fired up, drawing Braedon's attention to the van. Xavier was inching the vehicle away from the vortex, the machine straining against the pull. He managed to place the floating hovervan between his friends and the hole. With the majority of the gravitational forces deflected by the vehicle, Braedon let go of the beam and scrambled toward the van. He opened the side door facing away from the rip in time and space just as Charon and Jade arrived.

"Get in! Quick!" Xavier called out. "That thing's building up steam!"

Charon and Jade dove inside. Braedon paused at the entrance to the door, his eyes fixed on the body of Steven, still lying atop the vehicle twenty feet to their right. Because the car faced the opposite direction, it prevented the gravitational forces from ripping Steven's body from its resting place. But that wouldn't last long. Soon, both would be gone.

"We've got to help Steven!" Braedon called over the noise of the swirling winds.

"And what about Raptor?" Jade said from beside him as she stared out the window. "He's not going to make it!"

Braedon followed her gaze. Raptor had somehow managed to grab the same grate in the floor the Guardian had unsuccessfully attempted to reach. However, Braedon could tell strength was about spent. His face was ashen. The knuckles on his hands were white from both the strain and from his recent wound. The pull from the vortex, which was only twenty feet from where he lay on the ground, was now so powerful Raptor's body was being lifted slightly into the air.

Help me! Raptor cried out through his implant, his lips pursed tightly together as he struggled to hold on. He turned his gaze toward the van. Braedon appeared near the front bumper on the opposite side. His eyes scanned the area, no doubt searching for some way to help.

Raptor felt panic overwhelm him. His arm muscles were growing weaker with each passing second. *I'm not going to make it! I don't want to die! What if…what if…*

He screamed as his fingers lost their hold.

He flailed his arms, desperately seeking for something to grab. He slid feet first toward the hungry vortex. Its dark center seemed to beckon to him. It sought to claim him for its own. *Nooooo!* His mind shrieked.

His body suddenly swung around as if something had grabbed his leg. He cried out in astonishment and stared down. His pant leg had snagged on the handle of a screwdriver which had somehow become wedged in a grate on the floor.

Now that he was no longer sliding, Raptor turned his gaze in the other direction. He stared into the gaping hole a mere ten feet in front of him. As he watched in fascinated horror, the vortex began to change. The outer swirling edges started to lose their circular shape, while the inner core alternated between bulging and shrinking. Then, with a spectacular flash of brilliant color, the rip in time and space was gone.

21

PASSING THE FLAME

The disappearance of the vortex left an eerie, unnatural silence in its wake. The last of the loose papers and other lightweight materials caught in the swirling winds had settled to the ground before any of the survivors moved or even dared to breathe.

Raptor, are you okay?

His mind barely registered Jade's call. He was alive! Yet his thoughts swirled with questions, as if the vortex itself had taken up residence in his mind. They came and went so quickly he couldn't grasp one long enough to seek an answer.

He heard the door of the hovervan open. Moments later Jade appeared above him. She knelt and searched for signs of injury. Finding nothing more serious than the wound from the laser blast, she put her face close to his.

"Raptor?" she called softly.

He stared back at her blankly, his mind still struggling to focus.

"Raptor!" she said more loudly as she shook him. After two more attempts, he suddenly blinked rapidly and inhaled. He scanned his surroundings. The images being sent to his brain finally started to make sense.

"I'm…I'm still alive," he managed at last, his eyes coming to rest on Jade's face. "Steven said this would happen! It's the second sign!"

"Calm down," Jade said, unnerved by the wild look in Raptor's eyes. "Are you hurt?" she said as Charon and Xavier approached.

"What?" Raptor asked as if hearing her for the first time. "No. Nothing serious."

"Glad to hear it," Charon interjected, one of his thick hands holding a shop rag against a cut on his forehead, "because I've got this nagging feeling this place is about to become very popular real soon."

"Unbelievable!" Xavier exclaimed as he knelt next to Raptor to examine the tool that had saved his life. "You are one lucky gorge-jumper. I mean, what are the odds this screwdriver would happen to be just the right width, get wedged into this grate at just the right angle, your body would travel at just the right trajectory, and it would get caught in just the right spot on your pant leg? Maybe we should buy you a lottery ticket, because today is obviously your lucky day!"

Raptor glared at the man, the blood draining from his face. He felt the weight of Steven's prophecy return.

Xavier blanched at the response. "Hey, I was just kidding. It's okay. Sheesh."

"Let's get moving," Charon stated, completely oblivious to the exchange. He grabbed Raptor's arm and helped him stand. Together, the two wounded men hobbled toward the van. "I see now why Mathison's goons were keeping news of that Vortex weapon so hush-hush," Charon said. "Just think what even one of those weapons could do to an army!"

When they arrived at the vehicle, Raptor stood upright. His mind had finally cleared. It was once more time for action. "I'm okay," he pronounced to Jade and Charon as he stood without their aid. "Is everyone else all right?"

"Other than a stiff neck and a couple of new bruises, I think I'll live," Xavier said as he massaged his neck and grimaced.

"Nothing we can't handle," Charon said. "What's our next move?"

A sudden call from across the room drew their attention. "Steven's still alive! Someone give me a hand!"

Raptor and the others headed toward the damaged car. Braedon and Gunther were bent over the body of Steven and were removing as much of the broken glass as they could without injuring him further. Braedon glanced at Raptor, his expression dire.

"He's cut up pretty bad, and I think he's got some broken bones," Braedon stated grimly.

Raptor quickly assessed the situation, then glanced back over his shoulder at Charon and Xavier. "Go get two of the police cars and bring them in here. Grab a couple of their jackets while you're at it," he commanded. The two men nodded and jogged toward the open garage door. Returning his attention to his former mentor, Raptor reached up and felt the man's pulse. "It's faint, but he still might have a chance if we can get him out of here."

"But where will we go?" Braedon asked in concern. "We can't just take him to a hospital."

"We've got some friends who could help," Raptor said. "Jade and Gunther, go back to the van and get our gear and supplies. When Xavier and Charon pull the cars in, load 'em up. Braedon, that shelf looks adjustable. Grab it, and we'll use it as a gurney."

The two men took the empty shelf and detached it from the shelving unit. Laying it on the ground in front of the car, they gingerly removed Steven's unconscious body from the broken glass and set him on it. Raptor winced at the amount of blood on the side of Steven's head. A police car entered the garage and parked nearby. Raptor and Braedon opened the back door and carefully placed Steven inside.

The six companions had the two police hovercars loaded in a matter of minutes. Xavier and Jade donned two of the police jackets they had commandeered from the unconscious officers and climbed into the front seats of the first vehicle. Jade's pet mindim flew through the open window and landed on her lap, where it curled itself into a ball. Gunther sat in the back. Raptor and Charon put on the other two jackets and climbed into the second vehicle. Braedon sat in the backseat in order to minister to Steven's wounds with a med kit they had taken from the collected gear.

As the two stolen vehicles exited the shop and headed toward the open gate, the sounds of approaching police sirens wailed throughout the city. *Xavier, follow my lead. I'm going to take a few back roads until Inspector Hawkin's backup is behind us,* Raptor said via his implant. Xavier sent a quick acknowledgement, then pulled his car behind Raptor's. The criminal leader led the way down a narrow alley, closing the gate to the shop after them.

The echoing sirens gradually receded into the distance. *We're not out of this yet,* Raptor communicated to the other vehicle. *It might attract attention if you follow me directly. Stay here for a minute or two, then pull onto the main street. Meet us three blocks from The Pit. We'll ditch the police cars, take the secret tunnels to get inside, and get some help for Steven. After that, we'll grab one of the Cliffjumpers parked there and head over to the Vagabond Hotel. Aaron owes us anyway. It shouldn't be too hard to convince him to give us some rooms where we can lay low for tonight. Tomorrow, we'll get out of the city and figure out our next move.*

Got it, boss. See ya soon.

In the back of the car, Braedon had begun cleaning the extensive wounds on Steven's body. The sight of every newly discovered cut or abrasion intensified Braedon's prayers. He grabbed a syringe filled with liquid stimulant and shot it into Steven's arm. After several minutes, he stirred and moaned as he returned to consciousness.

"Hang in there, Steven. We're going to get you some help soon," Braedon pleaded, his voice hushed. "I've given you some stim, which should stabilize your condition."

Steven's eyes fluttered open. After several seconds of disorientation, his gaze finally fixed on the familiar face sitting on the edge of the seat next to him. "Where...where are we?" he asked, his voice nothing more than a throaty whisper.

"We're safe for now," Braedon answered.

"The Guardian?"

"Gone," Braedon said simply. "We escaped in two borrowed police cars. Don't talk. You need to save your strength."

Steven shook his head. "My fight is over, Braedon."

Although he wanted to offer some reassurance to the contrary, Braedon couldn't deny the truth.

"Find the way...back to Earth," Steven said, his breathing labored. "And...please...please try to save my...my family, if you can. Tell them...I'm sorry, and...I love them."

Braedon ignored the rivulets of tears running unchecked down his face. "I will. I promise."

Steven closed his eyes for a moment as a wave of pain passed through his broken body. He opened them once more and returned his gaze to Braedon. His eyes were glazed and unfocused.

"Raptor?" he managed.

"He's here, driving the car."

"You must…help him," Steven said. "God has a…a purpose for his life. Put your feelings aside. He is lost…like we once were." He paused to gather strength before continuing. "Be patient. He has many…many stumbling blocks preventing him from…taking the path that…leads to the…gospel. His personal pain…and anger toward God runs deep,…deeper than you could imagine. Let the Holy Spirit guide…your actions…and your speech."

Overwhelmed by grief, Braedon could do nothing more than listen and mourn as his mentor, friend, and surrogate father faded.

Steven summoned one final gasp of strength. "Remember what I taught you. Raptor has…many of the same questions you once had. But keep in mind…your goal …is to win him to Christ…not win a debate. Let your character…reinforce your words."

With his last instruction given, Steven closed his eyes, the lines in his aged face relaxing. "I'm…ready…Lord…" He released his last breath. The spirit that was Steven Russell departed, leaving behind nothing more than a broken, empty shell.

22

THE NIGHTMARE

His vision was shrouded in darkness. Disoriented, the man reached out with his arms to feel his way. To his left, he felt nothing but air. To his right, his fingertips brushed against cold, hard stone. He brought his left arm around to join his right and laid his palms against the wall. He leaned his body against the durable rough surface, its permanence like a lifeboat to a drowning man.

Feeling his way along the wall, he moved slowly forward, searching for something, anything. Where was he? Why couldn't he see? Was he blind, or was his vision gone because of a lack of light?

And why did he have this intense feeling he was being hunted?

He froze in place, his heart thumping painfully against his rib-cage. Was it his imagination playing tricks on him, or had he really heard a growl? In answer to his unspoken question, the sound repeated itself, only with greater volume. He had heard a growl! Whatever creature was producing that horrid rumble seemed hungry. And worse, it was getting closer!

The man moved with renewed urgency. He continued on blindly, his feet shuffling along the uneven floor. His breaths came fast and shallow as panic set in.

Then to his surprise, his eyes saw a faint light coming from somewhere in front of him. The light became brighter and brighter with each step. Hope spurred him on. He ran as fast as he dared down what he could now see was some kind of tunnel or cave. He stumbled in fright as another growl erupted from behind him. Regaining his balance, he ran toward the light.

The tunnel emptied unexpectedly into a large cavern made out of strange rock that glowed with a dark-purplish hue. In the center of the cavern was the object producing the light. The man paused momentarily in shock. An ornate jewel-encrusted sword stood erect atop a shining two-foot high pedestal. Its blade was thrust halfway into the solid granite. Multicolored crystalline light radiated from the hilt and pommel as if the weapon were alive.

Despite the sheer beauty and wonder of the sword, the man recoiled. Something within him knew that to touch the weapon would be folly. Yet he also knew with an unmistakable certainty that wielding the blade was his only hope for defeating the beast hunting him.

A deafening roar from behind sent him tumbling to the ground, terror piercing his heart. He turned and cowered at the sight of the two blood-red eyes staring back at him. An enormous shadow detached itself from the blackness of the tunnel entrance. Although his eyes couldn't make out the details of the creature's form, its outline revealed horns, wings, and a serpentine body.

Terror unlike anything he had ever known robbed him of his senses. He wept uncontrollably as he collapsed onto the cold stone floor. After several precious seconds, one thought pierced through the fog clouding his mind. The sword! He had to reach the sword!

The sound of the beast approaching infused his body with one last burst of energy, just enough to overcome the paralyzing fear. He crawled on his hands and knees toward the weapon. Yet the closer he got, the more he felt the pain of the blinding radiance emanating from it.

It was too pure. He was unworthy to wield it. The man curled into a ball and wept in defeat, his anguish bursting forth from his very soul.

He shut his eyes tightly and cried out in despair. He heard the beast behind him laugh—a horrible, throaty laugh of triumph. The heat of the creature's fetid breath washed over him. He retched from the foul stench of brimstone. The monstrous shadow paused as if relishing its victim's suffering. The man let out one last shrill scream of terror as the beast opened its toothy maw and devoured its prey.

Raptor let out a strangled cry and sat bolt upright in the hotel-room bed. Droplets of sweat were beading on his forehead. He remained motionless for several seconds as he calmed his rapidly beating heart.

"The nightmare again, huh?" Charon said from the other side of the darkened room, his voice filled with concern.

Raptor glanced at his friend. He tried to shake off the nagging sense of dread and unease that always accompanied the dream. He focused his mind on reviewing the day's events, hoping the mental exercise would serve to chase away the remaining vestiges of the nightmare.

After escaping from the shop, Raptor and the others rid themselves of the police cars. Since Steven had already died by then, they didn't have the added burden of seeking help for his injuries. They picked up one of the vehicles Raptor and his criminal companions had hidden around the city at various safe houses. After that, they headed straight for the Vagabond Hotel. Their contact, Aaron, set them up with rooms for the night. For a price, of course. They made arrangements to transport Steven's body back to his family, then settled in for the night. Raptor had collapsed onto his bed, his exhaustion carrying him into a fitful sleep. That is, until the nightmare occurred.

"Yeah," he replied simply, hoping his friend would drop the subject. However, Charon didn't seem to pick up on the hint.

"Look, Rahib, you've got to figure out what's causing this. We've known each other since before we were teens, yet I've never seen you like this. Even when we met—when you were still screwed up by whatever had happened to make you run away from home—you were never this disturbed. It's like… some kind of mental attack. I'm startin' to think Mathison's goons have come up with more than just a new physical weapon. Think about it, what if they could use that blasted Pandora's Box implant to put a nightmare into your head? It has certainly been robbing you of sleep and keeping you on edge."

Raptor paused as he considered the possibility. "Hmmm… maybe," he said, trying again to brush off the subject.

"That has to be it," Charon continued. "Either that or there's some glitch with your implant. I've read of that happening. There's this guy once who had to be locked up because he kept seeing images from a video game he played in the Box. He thought he was still in the game and tried to kill the people around him. The doctors said there was a problem with the implant."

"Great. So you're saying I'm crazy?" Raptor asked, his voice reflecting only partial sarcasm.

"Crazier than a cliff diver jumping into the Well," Charon replied with a grin.

The two shared a brief chuckle before Raptor's mood turned serious once again. Several seconds of awkward silence passed before Raptor spoke. "I don't know, Caleb," he said, using Charon's real name. "Do you…you don't…why do you think humans were brought through the portals here to Tartarus? Do you think there's someone or something like the Celestials pulling the strings?"

Charon frowned as he gazed at his friend. "Something really does have you spooked. That's a mighty big question to be asking at eleven thirty at night."

"Yeah, you're right. Just forget it," Raptor said. He laid down again on the bed.

To his surprise, Charon continued the conversation, "I don't really know, and frankly, I don't really care. If the Celestials do exist, then I've never seen any proof of them. I guess the idea of aliens transporting select people from Earth to preserve the human race because some huge catastrophe is coming makes about as much sense as any of the other theories I've heard. But as with all such beliefs, they're just that—beliefs. There's no evidence for any of it."

"What about God?" Raptor asked.

Silence hung in the air so long Raptor began to wonder if Charon had even heard his question. "What's going on, Rahib? You know where I stand, and I thought I knew where you stood. I don't believe for a second there's some 'all powerful' father God sitting on his golden throne just waiting to squash mankind if they don't follow his commands. All religions are just man-made superstitions used by con men to get people to obey them. It's all a power grab. Why would you even ask me such a question? And why would you bring it up? Does it have something to do with your nightmare?"

Raptor leaned his back against the wall and sighed. "Yeah, you're right. It was a stupid question. It's just…something Steven said back at the Crimson Liberty hideout."

Charon's frown deepened. "I thought so. You looked rattled when we were leaving. What did he say?"

Raptor debated inwardly how much to tell Charon. He'd been friends with Caleb for twenty years, and although they didn't always see eye to eye, they had shared many experiences together. If it came down to it, Raptor would give his life for him. But his hesitation in telling him about the prophecy stemmed from their difference of opinion about Steven. Raptor knew Charon hadn't fully forgiven him for running off to join the military when he was sixteen. He had always blamed Steven for taking away his best friend. A part of him was actually happy when Raptor was accused of murder and had to drop out of the academy.

In the end, he decided to divulge his secret and take whatever response Charon gave with a grain of salt. "When we were talking about the Vortex and Mathison, Steven suddenly became…weird as if he was hearing someone else's voice. He then began speaking cryptically, like he was reciting a poem."

"What?" Charon asked incredulously. "I told you. I never understood why you gave that guy any respect. He's a religious nut. I certainly hope you're not giving any weight to anything he said in that poem. What was it about?"

Although Raptor could remember every word of the prophecy as if it were etched on his heart, he decided to merely summarize. "He said something about the fate of tens of thousands resting in my hands. He said my fate was bound to theirs, and 'Only by opening the door to a new life would my own be saved,' or something along those lines."

"See! That's exactly what I was just saying," Charon replied in irritation. He got up from the bed, flipped on a small lamp, and poured himself a drink. "He was trying to control you by using religion. 'God says you should do this, and if you don't, bad things will happen.'"

Raptor felt his face flush from embarrassment at Charon's description of the situation. When Raptor had been under Steven's tutelage, he *had* respected him. He had respected his physical prowess and skill. He had respected his intelligence and wit. And he had respected his strength of character. Raptor had never admitted this to Charon, but Steven had become like a surrogate father to him during those six years in the military.

But Steven had changed since then. He still respected his physical skill and intelligence, but his character had come under attack. Even more, he had joined a group labeled as religious terrorists and extremists. Should he believe Steven's explanation or Charon's assessment? What was the truth?

The *truth*. There was that word again. Raptor thought back to Steven's journal entry. *What was the truth?*

"There's more," Raptor said at length, brushing off the nagging question.

"Yep, I knew it. Let me guess, it's something bad."

Raptor nodded. "He made a prophecy that I would have one standard month left to live unless I opened the doorway."

Charon shook his head in frustration and swore. "That just ticks me off. I know you thought highly of the guy. But to try to use you like that just disgusts me. Well, let me tell you something. He was full of it! You definitely shouldn't be letting something like that bother you. And frankly, I think we should wash our hands of this whole stinking situation. We should turn in 'soldier boy' and grandpa. We could get the reward money *and* sell the Vortex weapon on the black market. We could pay off my idiot brother and still have enough left over to live comfortably for a while. It's a no-brainer in my book."

Raptor swung his legs over the edge of the bed and faced his friend. "I would agree with you were it not for a couple of things. First, I've read the documents Braedon and Gunther retrieved, and I'm convinced they're legit. Second, you know as well as I do these guys aren't lying. You can tell just by looking at them. Gunther is totally out of his league and would have been caught long ago were it not for Braedon. And third, Steven gave me two signs that would prove his words were true."

Charon's body suddenly stiffened. "What signs?" he asked coldly.

"The first, he said, was already given. He said I would have a recurring nightmare. And before you say anything, let me tell you that Steven described the dream in detail."

Charon's eyes narrowed. "How many people have you told about this nightmare besides me?"

"No one," Raptor stated. "It's not something I care to share."

Although Charon remained stony and expressionless, Raptor had known him long enough to tell he was fighting his own unease. "What was the second sign?"

Raptor took a deep breath, then plunged ahead. "He said God would demonstrate his power by saving my life before the day was done."

Charon stared at Raptor in shock. "This had better not be some messed-up joke you're pulling on me. If it is, I swear you'll regret it."

Raptor chuckled, despite the seriousness of their conversation. "I only wish it were a joke. Do you see now why I'm on edge? Xavier said it earlier. What are the odds that a screwdriver would get jammed in that grate at just the right angle, and my pant leg would get snagged at just the right spot? It certainly messes with your head. I keep telling myself it's just a coincidence, but it defies logic." For a moment, Raptor considered telling Charon about the line in the prophecy mentioning the pain from his past, but decided against it. There were some things too personal to share, even to his best friend.

Charon shrugged. He downed the last of his drink and turned to face Raptor. "Look, the man you once respected as your teacher had changed. You need to accept that. For whatever reason, he felt he needed to scare you to get you to help open the portals back to Earth. Somehow, he was able to plant these nightmares into your head. After all, even *he* said the implants could be used to control people. How much easier would it be to put a recurring dream there? And the fact you had the dream before today means he has been planning on involving you for some time. That could mean that this whole thing is some elaborate trap, which only reinforces my argument that we have nothing to do with it."

"But how could Steven possibly set up a way of saving my life that can only be explained as miraculous?" Raptor countered.

"I don't know," Charon said in irritation. "He was probably working with Hawkins and planned some other way to 'save your life' that he could pass off as being 'God's intervention'. But the unplanned screwdriver incident ended up working better than anything he could have envisioned. It's not that hard to explain away."

Raptor was unconvinced. "But if Hawkins was working *with* Steven, then how come Steven's dead? That doesn't make any sense."

Charon swore again loudly as he slammed his hand on the table. The resulting vibration sent the empty glass crashing to the floor where it broke into several large pieces. "I can't believe you're still defending him! You still seem to have this unrealistic perception of the man and are blind to how he manipulated you!"

The big man walked over to the bed. He laid back down and shifted until he was comfortable. "I'm done with this conversation. You're like a brother, but you can be really stupid sometimes. If you want to help these guys, then you can do it without me. I'm done. Good night."

Raptor wanted to say more but knew from past experience he would have more success convincing a Box addict to give away a free session than convincing Caleb. His mind was made up, and now Raptor had an even tougher decision to make.

Knowing that sleep would be impossible now, he got up from the bed, grabbed his svith-scale jacket from the back of the chair, and left the room.

23

CONTRASTING WORLDVIEWS

Raptor left the room and took an elevator down to the main lobby area. He turned to his left and he entered the bar. The Vagabond Hotel served mostly middle-class clientele, and being located on the eastern edge of Elysium, they consisted largely of travelers who were entering or exiting the city. However, in addition to the legitimate crowd, the owners of the establishment also had dealings with several well-established criminal organizations. Underneath the hotel were hidden tunnels often used by smugglers and contraband dealers who wished to avoid the customs inspectors at the main gates to the city. As such, there was always a contingent of colorful characters milling about at any given moment.

As Raptor entered the area, he recognized several drug runners seated at the bar. Their boisterous laughter drowned out the ambient sounds of the various holoprojectors showing highlights from recent sporting events. Raptor had long ago trained himself to casually study his surroundings upon entering any room. In addition to the raucous group at the bar, there were several other smaller groups of patrons huddled together in booths, as well as a smattering of what looked to be romantic couples enjoying a night out. The only person of interest in the whole place was a man sitting alone in a booth near the back of the room. A gray fedora cast shadows over his face, making it impossible to see his features. Raptor recognized the hat as belonging to Gunther. *What's the old man up to?* he wondered. He made his way through the crowd toward the booth. As he neared the table, the man's head lifted just enough to observe who it was that approached. To Raptor's surprise, the face under the hat didn't belong to the old man.

"What do you want?" Braedon asked in disdain, clearly wanting to be left alone. The man's abrasive attitude grated on Raptor's already frayed nerves. Nevertheless, Raptor slid into the bench opposite the soldier. Braedon lowered his head once more and stared at the half-empty glass of soda in front of him. Raptor calmly ordered a drink from the holographic menu mounted against the wall. When he had finished, Braedon tried again.

"In case you didn't notice, I don't really feel like company right now."

Raptor leaned forward and rested his arms on the table. "Don't you think it's a little unwise for you to be out in public? Your face is still being plastered all over the holofeeds. Some of the people in here wouldn't hesitate for a second to turn you in."

"I'm not some rookie," Braedon shot back. "I know the risks. And I also know how to keep my face hidden. Why do you think I took Gunther's hat and coat?"

"That may be true, but you're drawing attention to yourself by sitting alone in the corner," Raptor stated as he sat back. "There are many who would take quick advantage of a loner. I don't think even your reflexes would save you."

"So what do you want?" Braedon grumbled. "Do you need something, or did you just come here to lecture me?"

"Actually, I didn't even know you were down here. I came to get a drink."

Braedon shrugged and took a sip of his soda. "So have you and the others decided what to do about me and Gunther? Are you going to help us or turn us in?"

Raptor smiled. He didn't much like the guy, but he at least admired his brazenness. "Jade and Xavier both want to help, each for their own reasons. And although this may come as a surprise to you," he added sarcastically, "Charon thinks we should go for the reward money."

"And what have *you* decided?" Braedon asked.

"Honestly, I want to turn you in also and be done with it," Raptor said nonchalantly. "But that would be the easy way out, at least temporarily. The good news for you is I don't mind choosing the hard road if I think it's in my best interest."

"And you're convinced helping us is in your best interest?"

"Yes, I do. The old man's data is pretty convincing. Quite frankly, I've kind of grown attached to my free will." He paused as a waitress brought his drink. Once she was out of earshot, he continued, "So I guess for the time being, Xavier, Jade, and I will be accompanying you on this little errand."

Raptor could tell by the softening of his features the man was relieved by the news. Braedon finished his soda and ordered another one before replying. "On behalf of Gunther and I, we're grateful for your help. And I'm sorry if I've come across as harsh. It's been a difficult day for me. I hope you can understand Steven was more than just my teacher. He was my friend and...and the closest thing I've had to a father since coming to Elysium."

Raptor was surprised at the twinge of emotions sparked by Braedon's words. They echoed his own recent sentiments and struck a chord in his inner being. "I get it. I don't know if you knew, but Steven was my trainer for six years."

"I wondered about that," Braedon said. "I noticed a similarity in the way you moved and attacked the Guardian. You reflect his style."

"So I take it he had something to do with you getting involved in Crimson Liberty."

Braedon nodded. "When I first came through the portal, I mentioned I was in the military back on Earth. The transition liaison signed me up for the ESF."

"Did you have any family back on Earth?" Raptor asked, an odd tone to his voice.

"Yes, a wife," Braedon said with sudden emotion. "If it hadn't been for Steven's friendship, I don't think I would have made it. He took me under his wing. He taught me, and helped me get over the emotional pain of being separated from my wife by introducing me to Jesus."

Raptor chuckled. "You make it sound like Jesus is a personal friend or something."

"He is."

"So I take it you don't believe in the Celestials."

"No, I don't."

"Why not?" Raptor asked in genuine curiosity.

"Because there's no evidence for it."

"But you believe in a God you can't see. Where's the evidence for that?"

Braedon paused. He took a deep breath, then let it out slowly. "Are you sure you want to hear my answer? This is a pretty deep topic."

"Bring it on," Raptor stated. "It's not like we're in a hurry at the moment."

"Fine. Then let me answer your question with another question. Have you ever seen Earth?"

"No."

"So then, how do you know it even exists?"

"This is a totally different situation," Raptor protested. "There have been thousands of people who have come from there, including yourself. They bring with them pictures, music, videos, and all sorts of evidence proving it exists."

"Granted. But still, you've never seen it yourself, have you?"

"Okay, no, I haven't."

"And I would argue it isn't different with the existence of God," Braedon said. "In fact, let me take this back one more step. How do you know *anything* is real or true?"

"You rely on your senses and use logical deduction," Raptor replied, Steven's journal entry still fresh in his mind.

"Right. Whether we realize consciously or not, we all make constant judgments about things we encounter or hear to decide if they are true or false. If we don't let our emotions get in the way and we think clearly, we do this much the same way a scientist would perform an experiment: we gather information, examine the data, and draw a conclusion.

"Let me explain it another way," Braedon continued. "Why have you decided to risk your life to help Gunther and I?"

Raptor shrugged. "Because I'm convinced it's in my best interest to do so."

"Okay. And how were you convinced of this?"

"Mostly by the governmental documents taken from the Research and Records building."

"But how do you know those weren't falsified?"

"Because I've seen enough real ones in my time to know a fake when I see it," Raptor answered. "These have all the markings of being legit."

"And what about Gunther?" Braedon pressed. "He claims to be able to open the portals back to earth. Do you believe him? How do you even know if he's really a scientist?"

"Because I did a little background check on the two of you," Raptor remarked bluntly. "And frankly, Gunther looks and acts like a scientist, and you look and act like a soldier."

"Fair enough. But how do you know we aren't spies?"

"Because no one is foolish enough to allow one of their friends to get killed in order to gain the trust of the enemy," Raptor said. "It doesn't make any logical sense. I saw the surprise on Gunther's face when he pulled the trigger on the Vortex. His reaction was genuine. And you and Steven risked your own necks to help what you thought was a Box-addicted nutcase. No. You're not spies."

"So you're convinced of the reliability of the government documents. You trust the authority of the information you received from the background checks—which matches what your experience tells you—and your logic confirms it. Right?"

"Yeah. What's your point?"

"The point is that this is the same process we use to determine if a worldview, or religion, is true or not. Each worldview attempts to answer four basic questions. The answers to those questions form the basic beliefs of that worldview. Once you know those basic beliefs, you can put them through the truth filter we just discussed to determine if they meet the criteria of reliability, authority, etc."

Raptor was silent for a second as he considered Braedon's statement. "I suppose the questions forming one's worldview have to do with what we believe about religion and the existence of God."

"Yes and no. A worldview is broader than that," Braedon explained. "The four basic questions are: First, where did we come from? Origin. Second, why is there pain and suffering? Evil. Third, what's the purpose of life? Meaning. And fourth, what's going to happen to us when we die? Destiny.

"When we search deep enough, we'll find we all have a basic set of beliefs that help us make sense of the world around us. These beliefs form the foundation on which all the decisions in our daily life are based. Unfortunately, most people don't even realize they *have* a worldview, much less think through the logic behind it. Let me give you an example. You believe in evolution, right?"

"Yeah. Don't most intelligent people?" Raptor asked.

"Okay. Correct me if I'm wrong, but you would answer the basic worldview questions as follows: Question one, where did we come from? In the beginning there was nothing, then it exploded in the big bang. Over billions of years, the material from the explosion formed the stars, then planets. Eventually the earth cooled and water formed. Chemicals mixed together and were struck by lightning, which created the first single-celled organism. Then over millions of years, that organism evolved higher and higher until it became modern humans. Then humans were transported here to Tartarus about two hundred years ago. Is that an accurate summary?"

Raptor grimaced. "Yeah, that's pretty close. But the way you put it, it doesn't sound nearly so scientific. I'm sure a scientist wouldn't explain it as 'nothing exploded' to create everything."

"Have you ever read any scientific material explaining the origin of the universe?" Braedon countered.

"Not really, but I know some very smart people who have, and I trust their opinion."

"So you're trusting someone else's authority. Hold that thought because I'll come back to it. Question two, why is there so much suffering? Well, if evolution is true and we evolved from animals over millions of years through survival of the fittest, then the problem of why there's suffering in the world isn't a problem at all. There's suffering because it's just the way things are. It's part of evolution. Right?"

"That's right. I experienced 'survival of the fittest' firsthand when I was growing up on the streets as a teen."

"But have you ever considered the ramifications of this idea?" Braedon asked. "If we're just glorified animals, then there's no such thing as morality. There is no right or wrong."

"Right," Raptor confirmed. "I'm not accountable to anyone but myself."

"So if someone were to rob you or kill your wife or parents, would you just throw your hands up and say, 'Oh well. That's life.' Or would something within you want to cry out for justice?"

The question brought painful memories to the surface of Raptor's mind. As he had done so many times before, he forced them to return to the cage he created for them. Braedon must have noticed the change in his demeanor, for he changed the subject.

"Let's move on to question three. What's the purpose of life? How do we fix all of the suffering? If evolution is your worldview, then everyone should live however they please. Our best hope for eliminating suffering is manmade utopia, which is exactly what Mathison is striving for. He's actually being very consistent with his own worldview. Do you believe Mathison is wrong in trying to control everyone?"

Raptor could see the logical trap he had fallen into, but knew he couldn't get out of it. "I see what you're doing. How can I say Mathison is wrong if I don't believe in right and wrong? Nice. But it's not that simple. Because he's infringing on the free will of others, he's wrong."

"But who decided that 'infringing on the will of others' is wrong? You?"

Raptor let out a chuckle. "That's my opinion and the opinion of many others."

"Are you saying if a majority believes something, that makes it moral?"

"No, but the majority will have the power to *enforce* their opinion," Raptor replied, his growing frustration coloring his words.

"All right, I don't want to belabor the point. Last question, what will happen to us when we die?"

Raptor grabbed his glass and took a long drink of the liquid to hide his sudden unease. After the day's events, this question was the *last* thing he wanted to talk about.

"According to evolution," Braedon stated, "the answer to this question is simple—nothing. If all that exists is mere matter, then when a person dies, they simply cease to exist. There is no afterlife. No heaven and no hell. As you said, there's no one to hold each of us accountable.

"The consequence of this idea is that, since this life is all there is, we should get as much pleasure as we can and reduce the amount of pain. In other words, we should live each day for our own pleasure. 'Eat, drink, and be merry, for tomorrow we die.'"

"That's a pretty good motto. I'll have to remember that one."

"Nice," Braedon commented dryly. "The problem with that worldview is that it's bad for society. Children, elderly, the handicapped, and other defenseless people suffer."

"That's too bad for them," Raptor said casually.

"I'm sure you'd feel different if you were in their shoes," Braedon said. Raptor smiled slightly at the cracks growing in the man's calm demeanor. Braedon continued. "We're all just one accident away from being handicapped. If that shot from the police officer had hit you just a few inches from your shoulder, you could have been permanently crippled."

At the mention of the wound, Raptor could feel it throb anew. He lifted his glass and took another drink to dull the sudden pain. "Okay, so you've explained my worldview pretty well. Now explain yours."

Braedon took a drink from his own glass before speaking. "Origin—God created the universe, including Earth. He created all of the animals and plants with amazing capabilities, but his special creation was mankind. We are so special, in fact, that he made us in his image. This sets us apart from the rest of the animals."

"I take it that's why most of you Christians are hung up on fighting against abortion and euthanasia, and you make such a big deal about the rights of the infirm."

"Exactly. In fact, the very concept that 'all men are created equal' is only possible with a Christian worldview. After all, it's kind of hard to be 'created equal' without a Creator."

"Yeah, well, that's probably why I never bought into that idea. So how do you answer the second question about suffering? If God is such a good God, why do people suffer?"

"Well, the complete answer to that question would require a lot more time to answer," Braedon replied. "The short version is God didn't want to create a bunch of puppets that would worship him because they were programmed that way. He gave humans free will. We chose to rebel against him, and the universe has been suffering ever since. In fact, Christianity is the only worldview that can adequately explain why there is such goodness and beauty in the world but also such horror and evil. Furthermore, we have a firm foundation for morals and ethics. Since God created the world, he decides what is right and wrong. He sets the standards based on his character. We compare everything else to his perfection."

"Making you into self-righteous hypocrites in the process," Raptor said snidely.

Braedon took a deep breath. Raptor admired his ability to remain calm, despite his attempts to goad him. "I disagree. If you understood Christianity better, you might realize that because we believe 'all have sinned and have fallen short of the glory of God,' then we believe we are no better than anyone else. We are beggars telling other beggars where to find food. Our self-esteem is not based on our own goodness but on Christ's sacrifice. Our worth is based solely on the fact that God loves us."

"If you say so. So how do Christians think we should live? Should we all give our money to the poor and follow lists of dos and don'ts?"

"Christians simply believe since God is our creator, he knows how we should act to live a life of flourishing. He wrote our instruction manual, and if we follow his guidelines, we can live life to its fullest. He didn't write the Bible and the laws to ruin our fun, but to show us the right path. We believe there are *moral* laws just as there are *physical* laws. We can say we don't believe in gravity, but we still face the consequences if we choose to go against it. In the same way, people can *say* they don't believe in moral laws, but if they choose to ignore them, they'll still be forced to pay the consequences."

"Like what?"

"Take sex, for example. God designed sex to be a beautiful way for a husband and wife to express their love for each other and as a way to produce children. But mankind has chosen to ignore God's design and use sex merely for their own selfish pleasure. And by doing so, they have to pay the consequences, such as disease, emotional pain, unwanted pregnancy, etc."

Raptor was impressed. "I have to say I've never heard that explanation from any religious person. Then again, I don't really know very many religious people, especially not Christians. And I certainly don't make it a habit of having deep philosophical conversations with them. In fact, I usually try to avoid the topics of religion or politics."

Braedon grinned at his comment. "I'm not surprised. Unfortunately, those are the two most important topics you can discuss. Anyway, ultimately, God sums up the question of how we should live by simply saying we should love him with all our hearts and love our neighbors as ourselves."

"Which includes giving away your money and following lists of dos and don'ts," Raptor reiterated.

Braedon sighed in frustration. "You're missing the point. It's not about what we *do*. We are forgiven because of Christ's sacrifice. We do good in response to his love, not in order to *earn* it."

"Whatever. I'm guessing your answer to the fourth question is that when you die, true believers will live forever in paradise, while the heathen masses burn in hell. Don't you think that's a little harsh?"

"Listen, Raptor," Braedon said, "I'm just trying to give an overview of the beliefs of Christianity. If you've got a few months, I'd be happy to answer all your questions."

Raptor's jovial mood vanished at Braedon's words. *"If you've got a few months…"* The words penetrated his soul. "Yeah, well, I'm really not interested in learning more about your religion," Raptor said abruptly.

Braedon frowned at the sudden change. "Then why the interest? Why were you asking me all these questions then?"

Raptor shrugged and took another drink from his glass. "For conversation's sake, I guess. I'm not really interested in any religion, especially not one whose adherents think they have a corner on the truth. I don't want to end up as a close-minded hypocrite."

Braedon took another deep breath. "Let me ask you one more thing. How do you define 'close-minded'?"

Raptor was growing weary of the conversation. His tone turned bitter. "Do I really need to repeat myself? You think your beliefs are true and everyone else's are false. You close your mind to other ideas and evidence."

Braedon seemed unfazed by the accusation. "If you were going to have surgery, would you want a close-minded surgeon? Would you want a surgeon who had studied and knew the truth about the body or one who was open-minded to other alternative methods that had been scientifically proven to be false? Or if you were on trial, would you want a lawyer that stood up in court and said, 'Ladies and gentlemen of the jury, I ask you to be open-minded about my client. Don't listen to what the eyewitnesses say and don't examine the evidence, just be open to these other theories about what happened that night.'"

"Nice try, but that analogy doesn't hold up. It's not the same. You're saying there's absolute truth, right? I read Steven's notes on the subject. But the problem with your analogy is that religion isn't something that can be proven scientifically. You can't prove personal beliefs true or false."

"No worldview can be scientifically proven. But the Christian worldview can be shown to be true in other ways."

"Really?" Raptor asked skeptically. "How?"

"Much the same way a jury can decide if a person is guilty or innocent. A crime can't be proven in the same way a scientific experiment can. A scientific experiment is repeatable and observable, but a crime isn't. It's a unique event that happened in the past. The best a prosecuting attorney can do is demonstrate the eyewitness reports and evidence support one conclusion. The jury then decides if the evidence is strong enough to convict the defendant."

"Wait a second," Raptor said, holding up a hand for emphasis. "Are you insinuating we should do the same with religion? But what eyewitnesses can you interview? What evidence is there for a belief system? That just doesn't make sense."

"But there *is* evidence," Braedon countered. "Every religion, every worldview makes claims about reality. Therefore, it's the job of every thinking person to use logic and reasoning to examine the claims of a worldview to decide if it aligns with what is real. Is the worldview consistent, or does it contradict itself? Is it comprehensive, or does it leave some important questions unanswered? Does it match what we see in reality?

"One should also look at the history of how the belief system came to be formed. When you think about it, these ancient texts are really like eyewitness reports. So we need to ask ourselves questions about them. Who wrote them? When were they written? Are they consistent within themselves? Do they match what we know about the culture and time during which they were written? Did the founder have any ulterior motives? You said you trust what scientists say about the origin of life. Why? Because you respect their authority. The same holds true with ancient documents. If they are shown to be reliable through archaeology and other sources, then this increases their authority in general. To sum it up, you need to ask, 'who says?' and 'by what authority?'"

"All right, you've made your point," Raptor said. "However, none of this really answers my first question: how can you prove the existence of a God you can't see?"

"But it *does* answer the question. If you study the great belief systems—Hinduism, Buddhism, Christianity, Islam, Judaism, Atheism, etc.—you will see they are all trying to explain reality. They are worldviews attempting to answer the big questions of life. I believe if you judge each of them based on their truth claims, you'll realize only Christianity makes sense of all the evidence. Only Christianity is internally consistent. And only Christianity ultimately makes logical sense. Thus, it proves God exists."

Raptor felt his lip curl in derision. "Those are some pretty weighty claims."

"The bottom line, Raptor, is that the worldview we choose ultimately determines the course of our life. It creates the foundation upon which all other decisions are made. Most importantly, we need to answer the question of what will happen to us when we die, for the answer to that question will tell us how we should live."

The last statement left a bitter taste in Raptor's mouth. He picked up his drink and finished it, hoping the liquid would flush more than just his pallet. He set the glass down, placed his thumb on the reader to pay his bill, and stood. "I appreciate the 'five-point lecture,' and I'm mildly impressed. Steven obviously succeeded in indoctrinating you. However, I'm really not interested in researching what different religions teach. What's the point when I don't even believe in God at all. Besides, you may have noticed I'm not exactly in a position to do an intense net search right now."

"Believe me, I understand. However, I would encourage you not to brush it off. Would you be willing to bet your soul that you're right? Are you really that convinced there is no God? If I were you, I'd make it more of a priority, *especially* considering our current predicament. After all, none of us knows the day or the hour that we'll die."

Raptor stiffened. Unnerved by Braedon's words, he forced himself to offer his companion a final unnatural grin. "Thanks. I'll keep that in mind. I suggest you get some rest. We're going to have a long ride ahead of us tomorrow."

Raptor turned and walked briskly toward the exit. Not wanting to return to his room, he chose to go outside for a walk to clear his head. He'd come to the bar seeking to forget his nightmare, yet the questions and arguments Braedon raised only served to create within his tortured mind a different kind of nightmare—one that pursued him relentlessly as he left the hotel and strode down the mostly empty streets of Elysium.

24

LEAVING THE CITY

Braedon stared out the window of the Cliffjumper as it glided along quietly in the tunnel. He was so enveloped with his own thoughts and memories he was completely oblivious to the conversation being held in the front of the truck. Since the heavy-duty utility vehicle could fit up to eight passengers, the six of them had room to spare, even considering their supplies and equipment. Charon, who had changed his mind about coming with them, drove, while Raptor sat in the passenger seat. Jade and Xavier were in the middle, and he and Gunther were in the rear seats. He glanced over at the scientist sitting next to him, wondering if he too felt like a prisoner. Although Raptor and his co-conspirators had offered to help try to open the portals back to Earth, Braedon wondered if there wasn't some ulterior motive.

Braedon looked out the window and pulled up the collar of jacket to ward off an imagined chill that ran through his body. He fingered the zipper of his jacket as he thought back on all that had transpired. Ten years had passed since he arrived in Elysium. His life on Earth seemed like nothing more than a wonderful dream. Even the faces of his wife, Catrina, and his mother and brother had faded with the passage of time. His stomach cramped tightly as he tried to envision them. *Maybe, just maybe, if this journey is successful, I'll see them again,* he thought. *I can make it up to Cat. I was such a fool back then.*

The tiny sliver of hope was under constant assault by numerous pessimistic thoughts about what obstacles might still lie ahead. *Will we be able to make it to Dehali, or will we get caught before we get there? Will Raptor and his companions eventually betray Gunther and me? Did his friend Travis make it to Dehali? Will we be able to find him? Will they be able to get the Vortex to open the portals? When will the war start?*

"We're approaching the end of the tunnel," Charon announced. "We should make it to the edge of the main road in another minute, leaving that 'shining jewel known as Elysium' in the dust."

His words turned Braedon's thoughts away from the unknown and toward the events from that morning. As their small group was preparing to leave, Charon approached Raptor and informed him he had decided to come after all. Braedon did his best to hide his disappointment at the news, but he knew Raptor saw it. The man's hostility toward the two outsiders was palpable, and his presence only served to heighten Braedon's already elevated stress levels.

The Cliffjumper slowed as it approached the end of the tunnel. Charon kept the truck at a slow crawl while Raptor transmitted the proper code to the door. Despite Braedon's misgivings about relying on these criminals, he wondered how he and Gunther could've possibly escaped the city undetected without them. Braedon had overheard snippets of conversation between Raptor and Charon. According to them, there were several of these access tunnels leading into and out of Elysium, all of which were kept secret from the general public. Few even knew they existed, and only those with the right connections could use them.

"All clear," Raptor said. Charon hit the accelerator and drove the Cliffjumper out of the tunnel. The vehicle turned a corner and passed between two rocky outcroppings before merging onto the main road.

Braedon saw Gunther's eyes widen. From this vantage point, they could see the entire city of Elysium.

The Globe was just rising in the east, spreading its early morning light throughout the entire massive cavern. The shining purple walls of the underground world seemed alive as they reflected the rays from the man-made device. The road on which the Cliffjumper traveled stretched toward the eastern wall. Behind them, it continued west for several miles before turning north to cross the magnificent Elysium bridge. A wide, silvery river flowed beneath the shining golden structure. The water seemed to sparkle and glisten with color and light. It ran parallel to the road until finally passing under another bridge as it neared the eastern wall.

"I take it you've never seen the city from out here," Braedon said. "It's quite a sight, huh?"

Gunther simply nodded, still in awe at the beauty. After several more moments, he turned to face Braedon. "I've always felt Elysium was a prison. I've tried for so long to find a way out, I never stopped to consider its full beauty."

"That's a common feeling," Braedon replied, "especially amongst 1st Geners. According to the historians, that's why there's been so much debate over the names of places. Did you ever see the holovid about the naming of Tartarus?"

"No," Gunther said curiously. "I remember the people in the Welcome Center told me something about it when I first arrived, but I was in so much shock I didn't really retain anything."

"They say that the First Colony spent their entire lives trying to get back to Earth. Like you and me, they felt this place was a prison. So they named it 'Tartarus,' after the prison of the underworld in classical mythology. They also called the river 'Styx,' which was the river that supposedly led the dead to the underworld. To them, this world is hell, a place of torment.

"However, their children, who had been born and raised in Tartarus, decided to give up searching for a way back to Earth and chose to build a life here," Braedon continued. "Fights and skirmishes would often break out between those still arriving from Earth through the portals and the 2nd and 3rd Geners. Over the years, those who were native to Tartarus began to resent the idea that their home was a prison and wanted to change the names. But by that time, Tartarus and Styx had become ingrained in the culture. When the city was built by the native-borns, they wanted a positive name to reflect its beauty and majesty."

Gunther let out a loud harrumph. "So they settled on Elysium, the name for 'paradise' or 'heaven' in mythology. I'd always wondered why there was such a contrast between the names. How interesting. I have to admit, the purple coloring in the rock is quite marvelous. And the way the fish and other creatures in the river produce their own colorful bioluminescence is spectacular."

Gunther his expression became serious and he lowered his voice to a whisper. "Tell me honestly, Braedon. Do you think we have any chance of succeeding? And do you really think Raptor and his crew are going to help us, or do they have some other motive?"

Braedon stared at the older man. Clearly he wasn't the only one being plagued by doubt. "I've been living in Tartarus now for ten years. I had given up hope on ever seeing my wife again. Then, just when I'd finally come to grips with that reality, you show up. I know you don't believe in God, but I have to tell you I'm convinced I'm following the path he has laid before me. I don't know what lies at the end of it, but I can tell you this: He is with us."

Gunther tried to smile, but it wilted into a grimace. "You know, there truly are times I wish I believed in God. I wish I could believe there is a purpose to life—a 'path' being set out by an intelligence who has my best interest in mind. Unfortunately, I don't believe," he finished matter-of-factly. He turned to look out the window once more. His gaze fixed upon the city which had been his home for the past five years. "No. I don't believe."

Braedon sighed and offered up a silent prayer. *Lord, help me. I'm surrounded by those who don't acknowledge you. Help me stand firm. How can I do this by myself? I'm alone...* His heart ached as his thoughts turned once more to his missing mentor. Steven's absence left him hollow. Yet even in the midst of his renewed grief, he felt a sudden assurance. Meeting Gunther was no coincidence. And, though he didn't want to admit it, neither was his meeting Raptor and his gang.

As he watched the city of Elysium fade from view, he felt his uncertainty lift. *No, I was wrong. I'm not alone...*

EPILOGUE

Taj El-Mofty stared at the beautifully crafted mosaic adoring the wall of the imam's private room. Although he'd been here numerous times, the way in which the artist had woven the calligraphy reciting a text of the Qur'an into the geometric shapes never ceased to capture his attention.

The door to the room opened, drawing Taj's attention away from the mosaic. His heart leapt into his throat in excitement as the holy man stepped inside. The Imam was dressed in an embroidered solid gray kurta shirt with matching pants. His head was adorned in a traditional white taqiyah hat rimmed with gold which contrasted sharply with his dark, full beard and mustache. Before the door had even closed completely, Taj crossed over to the man. The news he had to share was nearly bursting from within him.

"Asalaam alaykum," Taj said in greeting as he shook the Imam's right hand.

"Alaykum asalaam." The Imam walked to one of the two red-gold couches filling the center of the room and sat. "What news do you bring that is so important you had to see me immediately after the noon prayers?"

Taj took a deep breath to calm himself. "Ya Mu'aleem, we just received word from our informant in Elysium that a scientist and former government guard have stolen a secret weapon from Mathison's research facility."

The Imam's right eyebrow rose at the report. "What kind of weapon?"

"He doesn't know. But he believes, based on his source, the weapon can produce great power. He also said it might be used to stabilize the portals, thus opening the way back to earth!"

"And where is this scientist now?"

"He is headed toward Dehali to meet with a colleague."

The Imam stood and began pacing the room. "We must have this weapon. This is the sign we have been waiting for. The men are ready, our plans are in place, and now…this gift!" He turned and stared at Taj. "Take some men to Dehali and find this scientist. We need to discover what this weapon can do, and if it can indeed open the doorway back to Earth. We will then wipe out the infidels here in Jaheem and return to Earth triumphant! Perhaps the presence of our army and technology on Earth will usher in the reign of the twelfth Imam!"

"Imam Ahmed, there is one more bit of information you will find of great interest," Taj El-Mofty said, his voice laced with adrenaline.

The Islamic leader turned to face his general, his expression filled with intense curiosity. "Yes?"

"The scientist and his soldier friend are being aided by a certain criminal and his companions," Taj reported.

The Imam frowned. "And why is this of interest?"

"The criminal's code name is Raptor," Taj announced. "But his real name is Rahib Ahmed. Your son!"

AFTERWORD

At some point in each of our lives, we have to ask ourselves, "What do I believe?" and "Why do I believe it?" Often, the first question is fairly easy to answer. We have certain beliefs we've gathered over time, almost as if through osmosis. But the second question is much harder to answer. Why do we believe what we believe? Most people, if they are honest, will answer, "Because that's what I was taught."

But is that really a good answer? What if we were taught wrong? What if our teacher, usually our parents, was wrong? If so, how do we know what is right? By what criteria do we determine the truth of something?

Every day we hear news stories. Coworkers and friends share events happening to them. We receive e-mails from people giving us information, etc. In each of these cases, we have to decide if we are going to believe what we read or are told. But how do we decide? We do it in much the same way a jury would decide the guilt or innocence of the accused in a court case, albeit in a much less formal setting.

Arguably the biggest factor is the source. If the source is a friend or family member, we almost instantly believe the story. But what happens if the trustworthiness of the source is in question? In that case, we have to do a bit more digging. In addition to seeking out evidence for the reliability of the person, we would also need to ask other questions, such as the ones Braedon brought up in chapter 23. Does the story make sense? Is the story internally consistent? Does the source have a motive for lying? Do other witnesses or evidence corroborate the story?

As you may have already guessed, the other three books in *The Tartarus Chronicles* will deal with each of these questions as they pertain to belief systems, religions, and worldviews. For the purpose of this Afterword, I want to go in another direction.

To even have a rational debate on the issue of what is true, you have to first presuppose there is a truth worth pursuing. In other words, truth has to be absolute. It cannot be relative.

In past decades, speakers could give presentations and debates to audiences who would challenge the beliefs of the presenter. But in recent times, audiences will sit attentively and listen to a presenter, clap politely when he/she is finished, and leave quietly at the end. The reason for this change is that our young people today are being taught truth is relative. "What is true for you may not be true for me." With that mindset, there is no reason to debate anything.

This issue is often seen when people use the word "tolerance". According to the Online Oxford Dictionary, "tolerant" is defined as "showing willingness to allow the existence of opinions or behavior that one does not necessarily agree with." However, many alter this definition slightly to also mean "acceptance" of those opinions or behaviors as equal to one's own. The difference is subtle, but has enormous implications.

For example, let's say I have a friend who is a Hindu. I may believe Hinduism is not the truth, but he's still my friend and I treat him with respect. If given an opportunity, I would try to have a conversation about my beliefs in order to win him over to my way of thinking, since I believe it to be the truth. Therefore, I am being tolerant in the original sense.

Under the new definition of tolerance, I would have to also say his beliefs are equally as valid and "true" as my own Christian beliefs. If I were to claim his beliefs are wrong and my beliefs are correct, then I would be labeled as "intolerant." But consider carefully the worldview underlying that definition: all religions are man-made belief systems, and as such, none of them are ultimately true or false. All are equal.

What is really at stake is the very idea of truth itself. In this example, Christianity and Hinduism are making contrasting claims about truth. So the new definition of "intolerance" would be akin to stating I'm a bigot because my belief that gravity prevents a person from flying is offensive to those who want to fly! In the same way, a person might call me a bigot because I believe that accepting the free gift of salvation offered by Jesus is the only way to salvation. However, just because a belief might be disagreeable to someone doesn't mean it isn't true. Its truth or falsehood should be determined by analyzing its claims, not by observing the feelings it evokes in someone.

Unfortunately, many people don't realize this error. Instead, they let their feelings take over. They resort to name-calling without offering logical reasons why they believe a certain worldview to be true or false. They use inflammatory terms rather than coming up with well-thought-out arguments to prove a point. Some recent authors have claimed that to teach a child about religion is akin to child abuse. This is not a reasoned argument proving the truth or falsehood of Christianity. Instead, it serves only to inflame feelings of injustice.

Another common phrase used in regards to tolerance is, "You shouldn't force your beliefs on others." However, when you consider this statement carefully, you will see it is self-refuting. The person making the statement is doing the very thing he/she states shouldn't be done! If people truly believed it was wrong to impose beliefs on other people, they wouldn't impose their own beliefs on you by telling you not to impose your beliefs!

It is a sad reality that many people don't seek answers to the big questions in life until it's too late. They go through life with a belief system that, if examined closely, would reveal glaring inconsistencies. Take for example the moral atheist. In recent years, atheist groups have placed billboards in various cities at Christmastime with slogans such as, "Be good for goodness sake," or "You can be good without God." However, these slogans are making an important yet common mistake: the question is not whether one *can* be good apart from God, but rather *on what basis* should one be good apart from God? An atheist has no logical ground for acting in a moral way, since in his/her eyes, there is no lawgiver.

Let me give you an example made popular by writer Frank Peretti. Imagine a school playground teeming with children. They are, for the most part, playing well with each other and sharing the equipment—balls, jump ropes, etc. Why? Because the teacher is standing there watching everything the kids are doing and making sure they follow the "playground rules," which are posted on a big sign on the wall. In addition, the teacher will discipline any students who break the rules by making them stand against the wall, thus losing playtime.

But what would happen if, one day, the teacher wasn't there? For a while, the kids would probably play as they always had. But then, when it comes time for little Jimmy to give the ball up so another child can play with it, Jimmy decides he wants to keep it. The other kids yell, "That's not fair! You've got to follow the rules!" To which Jimmy replies, "Who says? Are you gonna make me?"

When the other kids see that Jimmy didn't follow the rules and didn't face any consequences, the playground atmosphere quickly deteriorates. Before long, everyone is pushing, shoving, taking things from each other, etc. And who rules the playground? The biggest, meanest kid. Thus, you have survival of the fittest.

In the same way, when God is removed from the picture, then there's no longer a moral absolute with which to measure behavior. Atheists may still be moral people, but they no longer have the *authority* upon which to base that morality. It becomes completely subjective. They must live inconsistent with their beliefs.

On the flip side, Christians act inconsistent with their beliefs when they *don't* love their neighbors. There are many Christians who violate the teachings of Jesus and sin in numerous ways, and many later ask for forgiveness for doing so. It's not a matter of how we *do* act, but how we *ought* to act; we need to follow what is true. Then, once we have discovered the truth, we are to do our best to align ourselves to it. Our beliefs should be reflected in our behavior, but that isn't always the case. However, we should always do our best to ground our beliefs in solid reasoning anyway.

As I've proposed in this novel (particularly chapter 23), we should carefully examine the truth claims of each religion and seek to determine which is true. It is my belief, based on my own research into the subject, that of all religions in the world, Christianity best matches reality and can be defended logically and historically. Christianity is unique among the religions of the world, and it is my goal over the course of *The Tartarus Chronicles* to show how and why.

If you aren't a Christian, I implore you to consider the claims of Christianity seriously. I would recommend books such as *The Case for Christ* by Lee Strobel or *Evidence that Demands a Verdict* by Josh McDowell. Both authors were atheists who set out to disprove Christianity, only to have their beliefs changed after reviewing the overwhelming evidence confirming it. For other helpful resources, see the suggested resources page at the back of this book. May God bless you as you seek the truth.

Seek and you will find.

Keith A. Robinson
October 2012

Suggested Resources

Books

The Case for Christ by Lee Strobel
The Case for Faith by Lee Strobel
The Case for a Creator by Lee Strobel
Evidence That Demands a Verdict by Josh McDowel
World Religions in a Nutshell by Ray Comfort

Websites

www.apologeticsfiction.com—the official website for Keith A. Robinson.

www.apologetics315.com—a great hub listing other apologetics websites, podcasts, and articles.

www.probe.org—the website for Probe Ministries. Full of great articles and materials.

www.leestrobel.com—the official website for Lce Strobel. Also full of great videos, articles, etc.

www.answersingenesis—although this website has mostly articles that deal with creation/evolution, there are many other great videos and articles available on a variety of topics regarding Christianity.

www.livingwaters.com—the website for Ray Comfort and Kirk Cameron's ministry.

ABOUT KEITH A. ROBINSON

Keith Robinson has dedicated his life to teaching others how to defend the Christian faith. He is a public speaker and author of apologetics fiction—a new genre that incorporates apologetics into the plots of sci-fi, action/adventure novels.

Since the release of *Logic's End*, his first novel, he has been a featured speaker at Christian music festivals, home-school conventions, apologetics seminars and churches, as well as appearing as a guest on numerous radio shows.

When not writing or speaking, Mr. Robinson is the full-time public-school orchestra director at KTEC school, a professional freelance violist in the Milwaukee/Chicago area, and a graduate of the Colson Fellows program. He currently resides in Kenosha, Wisconsin, with his two sons, and a Rottweiler named Thor.

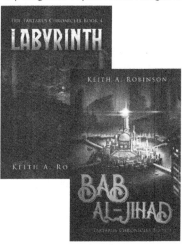

Made in the USA
Monee, IL
17 July 2023

38928647R00134